PRAISE FOR PATRICIA WESTERHOF

"Westerhof treats her material with a deft touch; she has an ability to show both sides of an issue with alacrity and understanding . . . Impressive." —*Prairie Fire Review of Books*

"In her first collection, *Catch Me When I Fall*, Patricia Westerhof weaves eleven stories into a sensitively imagined, multi-layered tapestry of life in a small farming community." —*MostlyFiction.com*

"Westerhof writes with quiet intensity and an anthropologist's eye. Her stories are to us a reminder that the ideological differences that threaten to divide generations have faces." —*Christian Courier*

"Westerhof gives a voice to these quiet people and depicts their struggle in finding their own voice against God, family, and their love." —*Telegraph-Journal*

"Westerhof knows her characters well, in all their braveness and brokenness." —Joanne's Reading Blog

THE DOVE IN BATHURST STATION

PATRICIA WESTERHOF

BRINDLE & GLASS

Brindle & Glass Publishing Ltd.
brindleandglass.com

LIBRARY AND ARCHIVES CANADA CATALOGUING IN PUBLICATION
Westerhof, Patricia
The dove in Bathurst Station / Patricia Westerhof.

Issued also in electronic format.
ISBN 978-1-927366-14-1

I. Title.

PS8645.E795D69 2013   C813'.6   C2013-901754-2

Editor: Robert Schreur
Proofreader: Heather Sangster, Strong Finish
Design: Pete Kohut
Cover image: AnnaGodfrey, istockphoto.com
Author photo: Camille Perreault

 Canadian Patrimoine
Heritage canadien

 Canada Council Conseil des Arts
for the Arts du Canada

 BRITISH COLUMBIA
ARTS COUNCIL

Brindle & Glass is pleased to acknowledge the financial support for its publishing
program from the Government of Canada through the Canada Book Fund, Canada
Council for the Arts, and the Province of British Columbia through the British
Columbia Arts Council and the Book Publishing Tax Credit.

MIX
Paper from
responsible sources
FSC® C016245

The interior pages of this book have been printed on 30% post-consumer
recycled paper, processed chlorine free, and printed with vegetable-based inks.

1 2 3 4 5 17 16 15 14 13

PRINTED IN CANADA

For Douglas

I said to my soul, be still, and let the dark come
   upon you
Which shall be the darkness of God . . .
So the darkness shall be the light, and the stillness
   the dancing.

—T.S. Eliot, "East Coker"

PROLOGUE

The Reverend Jacob Elzinga, February 1985

THE REVEREND JACOB ELZINGA BOWS his head over his type-writer and moves his lips soundlessly. He has told his two daughters that God hears all prayers, whether silent or spoken, because God can hear the heart.

The Reverend Jacob Elzinga's heart is large and compassion-ate. It appreciates nuances; it comprehends complexities. His parishioners who have sought his pastoral care revere him for his heart. *He understood.* Their voices hold wonder and hope. But the Reverend Jacob Elzinga finds his heart burdensome. He blames it for the paralysis that strikes him when he needs to make a deci-sion. What does he really want? Two roads open to him, both with attractions. And perils. He could stay where he is in southern Alberta. Wide open spaces for his daughters to roam. His wife's job at the Lethbridge Chamber of Commerce, a job she enjoys. A close-knit and supportive community. But sometimes stifling. Isolated. Narrow-minded. Or he could accept the call from Classis Toronto. Become the next hospital chaplain. Move back east. His heart tap-dances when he thinks of the bookstores. Tafelmusik and the new Tafelmusik Chamber Choir. The Hart House Reading Series. How he enjoyed the city when he was a student there. He imagines the collegiality he'd share with other ministers from his own denomination and from other churches. But he'd uproot his family. Winnie would have to quit her job. They'd wrench the girls from their friends, their school, the only home they'd ever known. And raise them in the city. That city.

If his own heart lacks conviction for either plan, the heart of God today seems remote, distant as the ghostly winter sun. He prays on. *Lead us not into temptation but deliver us from evil.* Outside his window the thin light ebbs and shadows stretch. *Thy kingdom come. Thy will be done on earth as it is in heaven.*

The prayer echoes in time and space; it hums as it joins the archive of all those—believers and unbelievers—who have petitioned God in their times of need. The Reverend Jacob Elzinga catches one of those echoes, hears it the way you glimpse something moving in the woods as you speed past on the highway. His mother praying the same words. But in Dutch, in a whisper. *Verlos ons van den boze.* Deliver us from evil. He stops his prayer and opens his eyes, searching his memory in the dim light of his study. She clutched him to her. The other children, all older than he, stood at attention next to him and his mother. He remembers, pictures himself, little Jacob, staring at their feet, the straight, unnatural line of bare feet on the cold, stone floor of the kitchen. The Nazi soldier pointed the rifle at first one, then the other. "Where is your father, boy?"

"I don't know. He left," his brother Berend says in a rush.

Onze Vader, Die in de hemelen zijt, uw Naam worde geheiligd, his mother whispers.

The soldier swings the rifle toward her. "Where is your husband?"

"He left us. I don't know." Her heart thrashes against his small chest. He can feel it, or maybe he is feeling his own heartbeat.

"Maybe I take one of your boys instead." The soldier's voice is sly. He points the rifle at Berend, then at Stoffel. Jacob feels his mother's body stiffen. *Iene miene mutte, tien pond grutten.* His siblings usually shoo him away—they think he's too little—but he knows how their games work, how you choose who is "it." He is straining to remember the next part of the rhyme when the soldier nudges him with the gun. His sister Beatrice sucks in her breath, a sound like the wind in the chimney during a storm. The gun presses on the side of his head, hard and cold. Jacob's arms encircle his mother's neck. He buries his face into his mother's skin. He smells the lye soap she makes, hears the clock ticking in the living room. "Little one, where is your father?" the soldier says. The slyness has been replaced with what sounds like tenderness.

"Gone," Jacob says. His eyes fill, not out of fear, but with the truth of his words. He lets one arm fall and turns to look up, and the soldier lowers the gun. "Achhh," he says, disgust and something else in his tone. Jacob's mother squeezes Jacob's hand.

The Reverend Jacob Elzinga switches on the desk lamp, a Tiffany lamp that Winnie and their daughters, Marta and Jennifer, gave him for Christmas last year. He inserts a piece of paper into his typewriter and types the address as it appears on the letter he has been clutching during his prayers. Classis Toronto, c/o Hope Christian Reformed Church, 27 Beaker Ave., Toronto, Ontario.

Dear Brothers in Christ, he types. He gazes at the words, then rips the sheet out of the typewriter. The Toronto churches have female elders and deacons as well as male. He starts again.

> Dear Brothers and Sisters in Christ,
> It is with great joy that I announce that I have been led by the spirit of the Lord Jesus Christ to accept your call. I look forward to taking up my new responsibilities with whole-hearted enthusiasm. My family and I will make arrangements to move to the parsonage in Toronto in July, and I will begin my hospital ministry shortly after we have settled in. I look forward to making the arrangements with you. The grace of our Lord Jesus Christ be with you.
> In Christ,
> Reverend Jacob Elzinga

He strokes his short beard. Toronto. Bookstores. Films. Plays. Traffic. Culture shock. Urban blight. He places another sheet in the typewriter. He's been meaning to buy a computer for some time—everyone tells him he'll love it once he gets used to it, but he's slow to make changes. He types the address—Classis Toronto, c/o Hope Christian Reformed Church. He types the greeting. His fingers tap, and the Smith Corona clacks; the carriage whirs each time he hits the return key. He almost hears conviction in the sound. He types,

> It is with great sadness that I decline your call to the hospital chaplaincy in Toronto. After much prayer and

contemplation, I have come to accept that my work here in Lethbridge is not yet finished. I believe that God has a leader in mind for you, and I pray for you as you continue your search. The grace of our Lord Jesus Christ be with you.

He rises to fold the letters and place them into two separate envelopes. He gets out his black pen, another gift from his family, and takes care to write the addresses the same way on each. He places the stamps the same distance from the edges of both envelopes. Finally, he leaves the room, shrugs on his parka and his winter boots. Marta is curled on the couch watching *Sesame Street*. He thinks about involving her—dropping the letters and asking her to pick them up or handing them to her as he finds his gloves. But this has to be between himself and God. His lips move like fidgeting fingers. He knows this decision is trivial compared with all the other matters in God's hands, yet he pleads for divine intervention.

The Reverend Jacob Elzinga trudges through the snow to the rusting mailbox. He shuffles the letters as he walks. *Iene miene mutte*. He stops, opens the box. Shuffles one more time. Places one letter in the darkness of the mailbox, the other in his pocket. Closes the box and raises the little red flag. Jacob moves quickly now, up the driveway, into the house. Takes off his boots but not his parka. Hurries into the study, closes the door. Snatches the envelope from his pocket and places it in the top drawer. Closes the drawer firmly. He will open it late tomorrow morning, after the mail carrier has been by. He will then see what his decision has been. What God's decision has been. He prays his prayer one last time.

Thy will be done.

PART ONE

WHERE WE START

And any action
Is a step to the block, to the fire, down the sea's
 throat
Or to an illegible stone: and that is where we start.

—T.S. Eliot, "Little Gidding"

CHAPTER ONE

AT FIRST MARTA THOUGHT IT was a cat when she saw it in her peripheral vision. An elongated, slightly deformed cat. But the way it moved. She swivelled to view it directly, and it curled its sleek head around at the same moment and looked at her, its black eyes friendly, if somewhat beady. The hair rose on her arms, and her fingers and toes vibrated. One minute she was dreading seeing Matt, wondering what state the house would be in, whether or not the neighbours had complained again about the garage, and then this. It had to be a sign. Sure, you could find wildlife in the city—eighteen racoons per square kilometre, she'd heard on CBC. And coyotes in High Park and the Rouge Valley, deer along the Humber. Skunks, squirrels, shrews, slugs. But a mink. A brown mink scampering along the concrete edge of the Toronto Island Airport.

The ferry glided forward, and a man's voice said, "You need to move inside, miss. This deck's for crew only." She reached for the handle of her carry-on bag, but her eyes stayed fixed on the break wall, though the mink had disappeared. She dawdled till the man's voice said, "Are you okay, miss?"

"Fine," she said. She turned then and strolled back inside the ferry, hardly registering its progress toward the mainland.

She thought the sign would be more obviously religious. She'd been looking for the face of Jesus, not a mink. Well, God moved in mysterious ways. She was Protestant, not Catholic—maybe God decided a mink would seem more affable, more accessible, than a supernatural visitation. She'd been searching for months now—since her friend Lily told her of her own little miracle. Lily had been hospitalized with flesh-eating disease, and her priest had visited and prayed with her. "He's had the stigmata," Lily had said with respect, even awe, in her voice. "He prayed, he blessed me, and then, after he left," Lily went on, "I felt peaceful, like I just knew I was in good hands." Marta had heard Lily's story four times now—it had become Lily's show-and-tell at gatherings, their friend Ashleigh's baby shower last month, for instance. Whenever Lily got to the "I felt peaceful" part, "He's Got the Whole World in His Hands" played in Marta's head like a soundtrack. "And then I got well," Lily said. "At an amazing rate. 'Miraculous speed,' my doctor said. 'Unusual in these cases.'"

Marta's own search for a sign had been a private thing. Mostly private. She'd told her sister Jennifer, but Jenn had snorted. "You mean like Jesus's face in a pancake?"

Well, yes . . . exactly like that. Marta knew about the eBay scams—people paying thousands of dollars, even tens of thousands, for a Virgin Mary likeness in grilled cheese. Those didn't tempt her—the artefact wasn't a real sign if you bought it from someone else; it had to appear to you personally. So she had found herself scouring the street as she walked down Dovercourt Road, pausing at puddles, scrutinizing the pattern of detritus floating on the top. Was there a face in there? Once, the cream had curdled in her coffee and gathered into an impressionistic visage. Against her better judgment, she called her sister. "Jenn, I think it's Jesus. You can see a beard, and the eyes are weird. So unusually kind."

"Oh, Marta, pour them down the sink. The cup of coffee *and* the container of cream!"

After she had hung up, the face was gone. Had drifted apart. Or maybe it hadn't been there at all.

Marta strolled off the ferry and strode out of the terminal to the parking lot. She had waffled over the decision to fly to Timmins just for a weekend. When her colleagues came back from trips, even short ones, they used words such as *invigorating* and *rejuvenating* to describe their experiences, and the claims struck her as inflated. Yet, she was feeling that the splurge of her trip, the relaxed visit she'd had with her parents, and the slower pace of the northern city had soothed her. Maybe she could bring that serenity into the week ahead; it could propel her like a tender breeze at her back.

The May wind was mild, but gusty here by the water, and it whipped her hair into her face. Her cellphone rang as she was climbing into a cab. She rummaged for the phone, bumped her head getting into the taxi, and fell clumsily onto the seat. The call display read Private Name Private Number. Could be Matt; might be Jenn. Six rings now. Marta pressed Answer.

"Hey, Marty-girl." Her husband was using his deep-timbre voice. Marta turned her head toward the car door so she could face an escape route. Too fast. A charley horse in her neck. Her tongue went numb.

"Hi, Matt." Excruciating pain. Tears in her eyes.

"You're back in T.O.? Did I catch you at a bad time? I can

tell I did. I won't keep you. How were your parents? Enjoying retirement?"

"I think so." She rubbed at her neck. "How are you doing?" Shoot. She had planned not to ask, not to give him an opening.

"Oh, up and down. Met with a new band yesterday."

"Looking for a manager?"

"No. Rehearsal space."

Marta rubbed her neck some more. The garage he rented behind their house was not zoned for commercial use or drumming late at night.

"But, hey, that's not why I'm calling. I won't be home when you get here. I'm meeting with The Wheat Girls."

"Okay. When will you be back?" Her voice sounded small, like feathery breath against a blast of wind. Marta pictured the two young singers, one blond, one strawberry blond, usually dressed in vintage floral ensembles, which made them look like little waifs playing dress-up. Men liked them, especially when Zara, the red-head, strummed guitar and Molly, the blonde, played xylophone, singing ballads and broken-heart songs in haunting harmonies. When Matt talked to Zara—when she phoned him, for instance—his voice slowed. Each word stretched a little, ending with a hint of suggestion. A small thing, not something anyone would notice, except maybe a wife listening in the background.

"Not sure. We'll probably go out afterward, hear some music. We need to talk tomorrow, though. You and I, I mean. I'm having trouble getting my share of this month's rent together. Waiting on payments from two of my bands. Can you cover us for this month?"

"I don't have the money. Not after this weekend's trip."

"Fuck!" A long pause. "Sorry about that. I'm a little desperate here. I didn't want to tell you, but I left my wallet in a cab last night. I'll probably get it back—I have a call in at the cab company. Driver seemed honest. But for now, I'm in a bad spot. Feel terrible about letting you down." He paused. She couldn't tell if he was lying. Sometimes he lied; sometimes he told the truth. It didn't matter; he used both deceit and sincerity to corner her, and most of the time she was helpless against him, fragile wings fluttering into a web. "Do you think we could borrow some money from your parents? The last time, I promise."

"I guess." She felt the sticky filaments wind themselves around her. One day he might paralyze her, and then what? She turned her mind away from that possibility and thought of the sleek brown mink. To her surprise, her exhilaration returned. Muted a bit, but strong enough to buoy her spirits. It had to be a sign.

CHAPTER TWO

THE SECOND SIGN CAME JUST five days later at Bathurst Station.

The morning was routine. Her fingers danced in her palm as she vacillated over whether to wear pants or a skirt, keep her straight brown hair loose or pull it into a ponytail, have coffee at home or a cup from the staff room later, walk or drive to work. On the last point, eventually, the spring sunshine inspired her, and, donning running shoes and stowing her pumps in a cloth tote, she strode first up Dovercourt, then along a mostly derelict strip of Bloor Street, past the empty Paradise Theatre, which had gone bust years ago, past a payday loan shop, a coin laundry, St. Anthony's Church, a psychic. She crossed Dufferin Street, then climbed the grooved concrete stairs of Dufferin Technical Secondary School. After greeting Amina, the guidance department office assistant, Marta shuffled to her office—Ms. M. Elzinga, Last Names *K–N*— and sat down to finish yesterday's paperwork before today's appointments arrived. When they did, they were the usual tangle of troubles—several students in danger of failing the year, a few whose irregular attendance patterns needed looking into, a pimply-faced boy whose English assignment hinted at violent anger, a girl just out of the Sick Kids eating disorder program. Feeling besieged, Marta listened, probed, scolded, cajoled, referred, made notes, and watched the day tick by. Everything was, in fact, so ordinary, and had been so ordinary all week, that Marta was wondering whether or not the mink had been just a mink.

She joined the surge of students exiting at 3:15 and took the subway to Bay Street, where she had scheduled a haircut. Not a haircut. A new hairstyle, from a hairstylist recommended by her colleague Chelsea in the art department. Chelsea with the tufts of platinum blond hair and a nose piercing. "Let Harlo cut it. Everything he does is flamboyant. You'll come out feeling like a million bucks," Chelsea had said. Marta hadn't so much wanted to feel like a million bucks. Her reasoning, foggy and indecisive, was that, if she had a stylish hairdo, things might be better. If she looked like Zara, the singer with orange wisps around her fairy face.

The consultation went well. Harlo, a slim man with tight black curls and a tidy goatee, was peppy and upbeat. "We'll show off your sexy neck," he said. She had flushed, pleased. Then the salon receptionist, a round woman with burgundy highlights in her orange hair, told him there was a phone call.

He came back, well, different. Marta crossed her arms more tightly under the folds of the hair-cutting cloak. Everything about him slumped. His legs sagged against her knee as he bent to cut her bangs; he held the scissors limply as he snipped at the layers. The hopefulness she had brought with her into the salon dissipated, fell away from her like the hair clippings that drifted to the floor.

Abruptly, Harlo put the scissors down and left. In the mirror, she watched him stride to the desk. Then he turned the corner, out of her view. Marta examined herself. Hair the colour of walnut bark had been clipped into uneven layers on her left side and hung limp on the right, one damp strand a cold wrapping over her cheek. Her hazel eyes, worried—the way they looked in snapshots whenever anyone caught her unaware—stared back at her. "You're a beautiful girl. You just need to smile," her mother used to tell her. By now, at age thirty, she figured her personality must have ossified, and with it, her habitual expression. The haircut was her only hope.

Marta picked up *NOW* magazine. She read the letters to the editor. Criticism of the mayor. Criticism of people who were against the new bike lane on Annette Street. She turned to the fashion spread. Today's model was a waitress who shopped in thrift shops and Kensington Market. A little bag lady, a little *Vogue*, a little prostitute. She turned to the "Missed Connect" classifieds and ran her eyes down them, with a forlorn hope that one might be for her. An attractive man who spotted her, perhaps as she waited at a red light on her way to the high school one morning. *Corner of Bloor and Dufferin. You: willowy brunette walking past the library. Me: blond guy in the Honda S2000 next to you, trying to catch your eye. You glanced briefly. Coffee?* Not that she was looking for someone—she was in love with Matt; that was one of her problems. But the attention would be wonderful—to know you had inspired such romance. Her eyes lingered on the last ad in the column. *Queen 501 Streetcar. You with emerald fingernails and strawberry hair. Your shopping bag tipped, and I caught your rolling avocado. Our fingers brushed. Dinner?*

Maybe she could paint her nails green, dye her hair red—after all, she was at a salon. And she could call the number listed—yes,

I'm the girl. She had never bought an avocado. Wouldn't know what to do with it if she did. This and the bad haircut she was no doubt getting made her depressed. Probably, she thought, she should leave. Refuse to pay. Find somewhere else and get another hairdresser to clean up the cut. She shifted in the chair, trying to find a comfortable position. Deep beneath the building, the Bloor subway train rumbled through—she felt the vibrations it sent up. It comforted her to think of it worming through the tunnels below like a fantastical beast.

Harlo came back looking even more morose. He fingered the layers on the left side of her head, snipped a few strands on the right side, and got out the blow dryer.

Once, when she was very young, in Lethbridge, her mom had sent her and Jennifer for a cut in the barbershop. "They don't cut girls' hair," Marta had complained, horrified. "Girls' hair is no different from boys' hair, and I am *not* going to pay double just because I've got girls," said their mom. She gave them money and sent them in, saying she'd be right back after she got a few groceries. They perched together in a chair and waited while the barber finished with a bushy-haired customer. The barber smelled like beer or whisky. He mumbled, his consonants slack and garbled. She used her thumb and index finger to show him how little she wanted off. "Just a tiny bit," she said. He said something about boys and long hair. "I'm a girl," she said. "I'm trying to grow it long."

"Long," he mumbled, cutting a chunk of hair away.

"Long," she repeated. She nodded her head vigorously as he pulled back to look at her. "Long." She still did this today—when students asked questions, she found herself nodding hard as she answered, as if willing the students to understand, willing them to nod their comprehension so that they could finish the transaction.

Harlo held up the mirror to show her the back of her head. It looked like torn lettuce. Like it had been sawed with kindergarten scissors. "Edgy," said Harlo. He looked uneasy. "You'll need to get used to it."

"Or other people will. I don't usually look at the back of my head."

Harlo laughed and patted her shoulder. "You're a funny one, sweetheart. Don't tip me. It's your first visit."

The subway was waiting when she got to the bottom of the stairs at Bay Station. She preferred sitting in the front car, watching out the front window as the train rattled and roared down the track. She liked the corners, the long, dark tunnels, the light that spilled toward them as they approached each station.

The bell signalled that the doors were about to close. She could walk to the west end of the platform and wait for the next train, or she could get on this middle car. She hesitated one more second, then raced forward and slipped through the doors, just as they were sliding shut. She sank into a seat, clutching her purse, worrying about the haircut—how it looked, how much it cost. The train stopped at St. George, then at Spadina; she gazed with glazed eyes as people departed and people boarded. And then, Bathurst Station. The doors slid open. A couple strode out of the car, and an elderly woman loaded with Honest Ed's bags shuffled to a seat. The doors gaped, and Marta looked out at the platform. A pigeon waddled from side to side, peering into the train. It looked to the right, then took two tentative steps toward the train. The bird glanced once more to the right, then, holding its wings slightly out, hopped into the car. Marta peeked around her to see if the other passengers had noticed it. A pre-schooler nearby was pointing at the bird with his chubby arm, his dad next to him nodding. The pigeon stood in the middle of the car, seemingly at ease. The doors closed and the train moved forward. The pigeon cooed. Its wings fluttered slightly. Marta had stopped breathing, stopped moving, stopped worrying. Her eyes stayed fixed on the bird, a rock dove—that was its proper name. She gave silent thanks to God for this sign.

At Christie, the doors slid open and the bird stepped off the train, moving slowly, like royalty.

CHAPTER THREE

"MEANING WHAT, EXACTLY?" JENN ASKED.

Marta tipped the two resin chairs on her little balcony and watched the maple keys helicopter down to the cement floor. At this time of year, the high brick walls kept the balcony warm and sheltered from the wind. A month from now, it would be too hot to sit here.

"I'm not sure." Marta avoided Jenn's scrutinizing eyes as she sat down.

"Mm-hmm." Jenn shifted her chair to face Marta's, then perched on the edge.

Marta leaned over, picked up a maple key, and twirled it between her thumb and finger. The stem felt cool and sticky. She should have prepared herself for Jenn's visit. Jenn asked questions for a living; it was her most refined skill, and the reason Marks, Didion, and Neiman paid her handsomely. When complimented, Jenn dismissed her talents. She told Marta once: "All the questions just boil down to, 'Do you have enough control over your insanity to be employed here?'" Marta admired her sister's knack for finding stable people who dedicated their working lives to the success of the law firm, but she felt like a zoo exhibit when Jenn focused the inquiry on her. She dropped the maple key. "I know what I saw." Her voice came out stubborn, like a six-year-old asserting her rights.

Jenn shifted her slim body in the chair, leaning forward with her chin out. She had shoulder-length hair, bouncier and a shade lighter than Marta's, wide eyes the same hazel as Marta's, but livelier, flashing with humour or, sometimes, impatience. "I believe you, and I agree both are unusual. Damn it, Marta, I'm not even saying they weren't signs. But if God is sending you secret messages, what do you think he wants? Or she." Jenn peered at Marta as though she were holding her fast with a beam of energy.

"I'm not sure." She should have kept the events to herself. She rubbed the back of her neck. Since the haircut had exposed her neck, she'd become more aware of her posture, worried that she was developing her mother's carriage, neck curving forward like a duck's. She moved her head back a smidge and folded her arms across her chest. "I have some ideas, but I haven't worked them all out yet."

"Well, let's hear them. Do you think you're supposed to leave your job? Or"—she lowered her voice—"your husband?"

Marta leaned back. The chair was cheap and uncomfortable. Someday she wanted all-weather wicker chairs with cushions from an uptown decor store. But Matt and his band friends would just spill beer on them. It was better to keep the little duplex they rented furnished as if they had a hoard of toddlers.

"Well, is that it?" Jenn's voice was a spotlight. Marta put up an arm.

"No! I think . . ." She paused. Her thoughts were muddled—unarticulated ideas like a lump of dough rising in the back of her mind. "I think . . ." She put her hands on her waist and rocked from side to side. She had no idea how she was going to finish this sentence. "I think—I need to find out what happened to Aaron." The words made her feel hurt and exposed. She bent over to pick up another maple key, wanting to slink away like an injured cat.

"You know what happened to Aaron. What do you mean?" Jenn's voice was still insistent, but Marta heard some hesitation as well. Two years younger than Marta, Jenn had been only sixteen when Marta and Aaron were dating. Marta wasn't sure how much Jenn knew, whether or not she was aware of the memories, the baggage that Marta kept packed into a dark cubby at the back of her mind. For whatever reason, Jenn, who loved to ask questions, had not probed there.

"I think I need to find out more details. How. Why."

"And this is what you think the signs are about? Opening up old wounds? Wouldn't it be better to leave that alone and get on with your life?" Jenn's voice was gentle. "Maybe you should consider changing jobs."

"But I like my job. Most days."

"Okay. What about your marriage?"

"What about my marriage?"

"You're not flourishing, Marta."

"That's not Matt's fault. He's just . . . better at new relationships than old ones."

Jenn didn't roll her eyes, but Marta knew her well enough to see she wanted to. Marta strove to keep the details of her marriage from her sister, especially the details that made Marta doubt him. She hadn't, for instance, told Jenn about Matt's "stolen" wallet. It had shown up the next day, missing only the cash Matt claimed he had been saving for rent. Still, Marta was aware that Jenn saw more than Marta confided. She squirmed in the hard resin seat.

Jenn's eyes were still on her. "You keep waiting for things to get better, but they don't. How long are you planning to wait?"

"I don't have a plan, you know that. I never have plans."

"You used to. When we were little. You always decided what we would play, where we would go." This time there was no question from Jenn. But the inquiry was there anyway, hanging in the air like a cartoon question mark: "What happened to you?" Marta felt she knew the answer.

MARTA GOT up late on Monday and power-walked to school, humming a David Gray tune. She couldn't remember the words, but the melody was stuck on repeat. She greeted a few subdued faces on her way into the school. Mondays were hard for students. Eyes bleary, feet dragging, they staggered in from the weekend, weighed down by the unfinished homework in their backpacks and the shock of the early morning.

Abdi Khalid was Marta's first appointment. From Somalia, she remembered. He sat politely while she pulled up his file on the computer. It was the first time she'd seen him since he transferred out of an English as a Second Language program in September. That he had attracted no attention during the school year suggested he had adjusted to the school fairly well, or at least that he was a dutiful student. She noted the seventy-eight percent average on his last report card. "I want to go to college or perhaps to university after next year," he said, a lilting thickness in his accent. "Have I selected the right courses?" She turned from her computer screen and looked at him. His brown skin was luminous, his eyes earnest. He smelled of some spice she failed to identify. Not unpleasant, just unfamiliar. Her eyes shifted to his T-shirt: STOP THE BUS AND LET MY BROTHER JACK OFF. The hand on her computer mouse picked it up and held it in front of her like a shield. She scrutinized Abdi's expression. Was there smugness there? A slight smirk? No. He just waited courteously. He had come straight to the guidance office, missing homeroom for his appointment, so she was probably the first staff member to read the shirt. He must not know, didn't get the double entendre. Somehow in his two years in Canada so far, he had missed out on learning that bit of slang. Maybe the ESL teachers needed to do more teaching about sexual terms and innuendo.

She turned back to the screen. She should tell him—before some other teacher sent him to the vice-principal. "Your courses look fine." She heard the strain in her voice. "We'll just switch you into the 12U English instead of the college/workplace one you selected. You need the 12U for university." She clicked the mouse for the course switch, then pulled up his schedule on the screen. "Let me check one other thing," she murmured. She clicked the mouse and looked at his schedule: Day one, period one, physics with Ms. Schutter. Ms. Schutter would kick him out of class, make it a discipline issue. He'd spend first period waiting to see the vice-principal, missing the lesson. He'd be sent home to change and miss second period too. She should just call the Phys

Ed department and get another shirt for him. But Abdi would ask what was wrong with his shirt, and she would have to explain what "jack off" meant, and her office was so small that even with the door open there wasn't enough room for the embarrassment the conversation would cause the two of them. She glanced again at the narrow shoulders, the thin chest. She cleared her throat. All those psychology courses, the professional training, yet she felt so ill-equipped. The office was so small. It was hard to make decisions in such a small space. She stood up. "Wait here a minute." She handed him a sheaf of glossy university flyers, then went into the office next door—Ms. S. Keith, Last Names *O–T*. Sue was in a meeting this morning; her office was empty. Now that Marta was alone, it was easier to think. She picked up the phone. A moment later she returned to her office. "Abdi, Mr. Jones from the Phys Ed department—do you know him?" The boy shook his head. "Well, he's coming up here to talk to you for a second." She felt her face flush again. "You can wait for him in the outer office."

Abdi followed her meekly into the reception area by the assistant's desk. Marta heard Ian Jones's guffaw in the hallway—that man always found something to laugh about. "I'll be in touch soon about a time for you to take those interest surveys," she said. She gave Abdi what she hoped was a bright smile. From now on, whenever they saw each other, they would both think about the T-shirt. As she turned away, she identified the song squatting in her head all morning—David Gray's "First Chance," the lyrics expressing someone's urgent plan to get out of here, wherever *here* was. She'd had a playlist of leaving songs in her head lately, old folk tunes like Paul Simon's "50 Ways to Leave Your Lover" and pop songs from this decade, like Kelly Clarkson's "Breakaway." She considered examining the reasons for the playlist, and warned herself to keep this detail from Jenn if she wanted to avoid further interrogation.

The administrative assistant, Amina, waved Marta over. She nodded toward a thin, sallow-faced girl slouched in the vinyl chair farthest from the desk. The girl was staring at the floor and chewing on a strand of dark brown hair. "Your next appointment," said Amina quietly. "Mercedes Lopez."

Marta glanced out the window behind Amina's desk. It was a gloomy day, the sky spitting rain when she had sprinted into school an hour earlier. She would rather wander out into the spit than return to her tiny office, she thought. Beneath her, the subway rumbled past, sending up its usual vibrations and noise. But now it made her think not just of escape, but of the mysterious pigeon. The rock dove. Doves were a gentle breed, symbolic birds. A sign.

"Mercedes," she said, walking toward the slumped figure. The girl looked up nervously. "Come into my office."

The girl examined the floor while Marta studied her. Marta didn't need to consult her notes—this student was fresh in her memory. The biology teacher had referred her. "The class was dissecting pigs. Pretty sure I saw cut marks when she pushed up her sleeves to wash her hands."

"How are you feeling, Mercedes?" Marta's voice was gentle.

"Fine." Her eyes on the floor.

"Mr. Lee thinks he saw cut marks on your arms. Are you hurt?"

Quick, frightened glance at her. "No. I'm fine." The words short and breathy.

"May I just take a look?" The girl wore a hoodie with tight cuffs around the wrists.

"No. I'm fine." Marta waited. The girl fidgeted, avoiding eye contact.

"That's great if you're fine. But I need to make sure because that's my job, to make sure you're okay." Marta's voice was patient and calm, the matter-of-fact way her mother had spoken to her when she was little and needed a shot or when the doctor was about to set her broken wrist. "You'll be okay. I'm here with you."

"I—I cut my arm on something. But it's fine, and you don't need to look at it."

"I know you don't want to show me. But I need to check that it's not infected and that you're okay. We'll just sit here together for a while, and when you're ready, you can roll up your sleeve for me. How are things going for you?"

"Fine." The girl's body slumped back again into the relaxed but defeated posture it had before.

"Your classes are going okay?"

"I'm going to fail math."

"Well, we can look into summer school. Other classes?"

"Fine."

"Things okay with your friends?"

"Yeah."

"How are things at home?"

"Fine." They fell into silence again, and Marta let the silence grow uncomfortable. Mercedes jiggled her leg. "Can I go back to class now?"

"After you've shown me your arm." The matter-of-fact tone again. Marta waited, resisting a look at the clock on her desk. The fidgeting sped up, the girl's leg jerking back and forth so fast it looked like a one-leg seizure.

After a long stretch of silence—four minutes? five minutes?— the girl looked at Marta, and Marta felt compassion for her—the pock-marked, plain face, the sad eyes, the sallow complexion—did the girl sleep? "All right," the girl said. She uncrossed her legs and held out her arm toward Marta.

"You want me to push up your sleeve?" Marta said.

The girl said nothing.

Stupid question. Marta reached over and gently moved the sweater up. She turned over the girl's arm. Horizontal slice marks ran parallel from just above the wrist to the elbow.

It was an odd thing, thought Marta. With situations like the one earlier with Abdi, she felt rattled; she second-guessed herself; she dithered about the course of action. But when someone like Mercedes came through her office door, she experienced a clarity of purpose and a rare confidence in herself. More than her training was marching forward to help this suicidal girl—it was as if her mind had help from other sources within her, the way one accessed the knowledge in one's fingers to remember lock combinations or piano pieces. She looked Mercedes in the eye, certain she could guide the girl through her humiliation at the exposure, past her shock at the intimacy of the encounter, toward help and hope.

"You've been having a hard time lately." Her voice was kind. Tears formed in the girl's eyes and watered her cheeks. Marta sat still, holding the girl's arm in her hand. In a minute the girl would be sobbing, her shoulders shaking with the impact of the encounter. "I'm going to get you some help," said Marta. The girl's stricken eyes held hers, terrified but holding on. "I'm glad you showed me this. You're not alone. I'm going to help you."

MARTA ARRIVED home to the booming of bass and drums from the garage and an angry message on their voice mail from Mr. Silva, the neighbour to the north. She sank down at the piano. It was a cheap instrument whose tuning drifted within a couple days of the tuner's visit. But it was better than nothing. She worked on her own song for a little while. Once—it seemed so long ago now—she had dreamed of being a famous folk singer, the Joni Mitchell of the early twenty-first century. The song was going poorly. She liked the initial idea, an extended metaphor about problems as knots only God could untie. But a lawnmower landed in the first verse and had plowed through it awkwardly for two weeks now. Probably she needed to throw this song out. She played the chords and crooned the words:

> My love is the grass you're about to cut
> While I watch you and pray for your feet
> Now you've run over the cord
> And I see that the Lord
> Controls knots and cords from his seat.

The ideas were clunky; the rhythm was off. Her fingers travelled the keys in familiar patterns for a while—piano arrangements of folk classics: Gordon Lightfoot, Kate and Anna McGarrigle. The melancholy tune in "Going Back to Harlan" made her feel restless. Or maybe it was the references to a frail heart and gallows, or the allusions to tragic love ballads in the last verse. She plunked out the tune of "The Ballad of Barbara Allan" and sang a few verses.

> Was in the merry month of May
> When green buds all were swelling,
> Sweet William on his death bed lay
> For love of Barbara Allan.
>
> He sent his servant to the town
> To the place where she was dwelling,
> Said you must come to my master dear
> If your name be Barbara Allan.
>
> So slowy slowly she got up
> And slowly she drew nigh him,
> And the only words to him did say
> Young man I think you're dying.

Something creaked in the back corner of her mind, and fear and guilt seeped forward. Stop it, Marta told herself. Think about today. The difficult meeting with the parents who want their autistic boy enrolled in a mainstream grade nine class next year.

A dozen meetings with grade elevens about course selection for next year, the important things she caught like a missing credit or incomplete community service hours. She thought of Abdi's shirt and blushed. Mercedes Lopez. The girl would be all right. The cuts were shallow and methodical—a sign of deep distress but not of a true death wish. She said a prayer for the girl, that the therapist would be capable and compassionate, that the girl would be honest and brave. This one she held out hope for. The ones that worried her were the ticking time bombs, the ones with real death wishes. The ones that left school in a black mood one afternoon and hanged themselves from their bedroom ceilings.

Her fingers played another verse of "Barbara Allan."

CHAPTER FOUR

MARTA WOKE TO THE ALARM on Saturday morning, and her arm flew to turn off the buzzer. Even so, Matt gave a disapproving grunt and pulled his pillow over his head.

The humid air mass that had nestled into the city the day before had produced heat unusual for May. Marta slipped on a light cotton sundress and covered her shoulders with sunscreen in case the line-ups were long. She and Jenn had negotiated their agenda for Doors Open Toronto on the phone last night, deciding to start with the ghost ballroom of a grand old hotel on King Street.

"This used to be the 'it' place for wedding receptions and glamorous events," said Jenn as they rode the service elevator to the Crystal Ballroom on the seventeenth floor. Her eyes gleamed. "The pamphlet says it's in disrepair, but its 'former splendour' still shows."

"Why did it close?"

"Fire regulations, I think."

Marta wasn't sure whether it was the elevator ride or her anticipation that felt like hummingbirds in her stomach. As kids, how they had loved poking around in abandoned and secluded places—deserted barns, the vacant lot near their house back in Lethbridge, the Oldman River culvert under the railroad tracks.

The elevator doors opened, and the guide marched them

through a short hallway into the pale yellow ballroom. "Wow," Jenn said.

Despite the peeling paint and missing chandeliers, the room shimmered. Light poured in through windows on three sides. The windows stretched from Marta's waist to the ceiling many metres above her. Mouldings shaped like classical pillars graced the walls. Though cracked, they stood erect, ornate, and grand. A balcony overlooked the room, its gold-leaf decorations glowing despite many years' neglect. "Do you want to go up there first?" Marta asked.

"No—more information there." Jenn pointed at the row of easels that held historical photos and newspaper stories featuring the room.

"I'll meet you back down here."

Marta climbed the wooden stairs. Leaning forward on the balcony rail, she surveyed the combination of magnificence and decay before her: the holes in the ceiling, the ruined surfaces, the exquisite trim. Doors Open had brought in a string quartet from Tafelmusik; seated in metal folding chairs, the musicians played a Mozart allegretto. It was easy to imagine the room in its glory, with extravagantly clothed people sipping cocktails or champagne, murmuring secrets in the corners. She pictured the dance floor filled not with the chaos and carnal gyrations of the school events she had to supervise, but with graceful couples who observed the propriety and the formal choreography of the ballroom. It struck her that her life lacked splendour of any kind, the thought a mosquito landing on her arm.

Marta descended the stairs and wandered toward the quartet, where Jenn joined her. Sunbeams caught the instruments and glinted off; the room danced with music and light. "They're really good," Jenn murmured. Marta nodded. Three men and a woman. The cellist resembled her instrument, a wide waist and bottom flowing from narrow shoulders. All the players were skilled, but the cellist stood out. Marta noted the articulation, the warm tone.

"Too bad Dad's not here." She kept her voice low.

"You're right. I'll take a picture to send to him." Jenn took a few steps back and aimed the camera. "Look this way and smile." Her whisper was a loud hiss that made the violinist glance their way. Marta turned obediently and donned as happy an expression as she could on demand. Their father loved Tafelmusik. It was one of his regrets when he had turned down the first call to Toronto, and one of the reasons he had accepted the second call. He and their mother had a subscription to Tafelmusik in the years they lived in Toronto, and Marta suspected he was pining for the orchestra up in Timmins. But Christian Reformed ministers rarely served in the same church for more than a decade. Nor could they apply for jobs; like storybook maidens hoping for suitors, they waited for a congregation to show interest in them. Marta's father was nearing retirement when the Timmins church sent him an official call. "I might not get another one," he told the girls. "Better say yes to this." Marta had nodded; it had never been the girls' place to question their father's decisions about which church he would serve. She remembered the disappointment she felt in Lethbridge at five years old when she found out they were not moving to

Toronto. Her dad had been reading *Pippi in the South Seas* to her, and she longed for adventure. She'd told him that, but he said he'd already sent the letter saying no. "Can't you phone them and say you changed your mind?" she'd asked. "No, honey. I haven't changed my mind." And Marta remembered the trepidation she felt at sixteen when her dad uprooted them, taking the family to Toronto after all. It was an awful age to move.

Despite the lively tempo of the music and the sunlight darting across the room, Marta felt sadness waft toward her. Jenn shifted toward the balcony side of the room, her elbows crooked like teacup handles as she snapped photos of the mouldings and the ceiling. Marta turned back to the quartet, and her sadness deepened. Feeling resigned, she accepted its familiar company, like a family member you make room for on the couch. She watched the cellist's strokes, tender ministrations, a love affair with the instrument. Maybe, Marta thought, if she herself felt that adoration for her piano—that intimacy with it—she'd be a better musician.

The allegretto concluded, and the quartet began a Haydn piece, a melancholy adagio that matched Marta's falling mood but seemed inappropriate for a ballroom. Marta meandered past a family taking a group photo and strode to the nearest windows, which faced east. The view was striking, though a bit lifeless from this height. Pedestrians were specks, obscured by rooftops and treetops. She gazed at the assortment of styles and ages of the architecture: the hundred-and-fifty-year-old St. James' Cathedral with its Gothic Revival design and the tallest spire in Canada; the mid-twentieth-century factories, mysterious chimneys and pipes jutting from their flat tops; and the contemporary apartment buildings, square and soulless. Lake Ontario glimmered a deep blue on the southern edge of the panorama, teasing her. Marta shouldered her way to the south windows, where many of the visitors had congregated to peer at the view. With relief, her eyes found the water and the distance it provided, a more open vista than the city stretching east. She rarely thought about the prairie landscape of her childhood, but when her eyes rested on a natural vista rather than the clutter of the cityscape, they lingered there, the space opening her chest, slowing her breathing.

She thought again of the ballroom awhirl with sparkling guests and dancers spinning to the music. "You're no fun anymore," Matt had said lightly a couple of weeks ago when she left the Rivoli before the band's second set. "It's a weeknight," she had replied. "I have to be up by seven o'clock tomorrow." But he was right. She'd been tolerating the parties, the clubbing, the concerts because she wanted to be with him. Had she been alive back when the chandeliers twinkled in the Crystal Ballroom, had she been invited to an elegant gala here, it would be the same; *she* would be the same. She might be dressed in brocade or velvet rather than cotton, but she would stand at the end of the room, at a window, staring out, staring down at the street, imagining leaving.

Jenn appeared at her side. "Ready to go?"
"Ready."

THEY WALKED a block east to the Flatiron Building on Church Street. The pamphlet explained that it was built as the head office of the Gooderham and Worts distillery in 1892. Marta had often studied the mural on the west end of the building, a century window that mimicked the windows of the buildings across the street: all elegant arches and wide, moulded frames. She'd admired the skill of the painter who'd captured sunlight and breeze in the portrayal of the white curtain billowing.

Inside, the foyer smelled of polished wood, air conditioning, and money. The building predated the school she worked in by thirty years, but it seemed both older and newer. It lacked the tired walls, stained ceiling tiles, and scuffed floors of Dufferin Tech. The renovations had added an Arts and Crafts railing, new walls, new floors, central air. What remained from the past were the red bricks and the elegant bones: twelve-foot-high ceilings, fireplaces, brass fittings, and wedge-shaped offices at the narrow end of the building. The guide drew their attention to the manually operated Otis elevator, the oldest elevator in the city. Made of gleaming wood and brass, it stood like a portal to an earlier time. "More impressive than the toilet we saw last year," Jenn whispered. Marta grinned. The docent at Colborne Lodge in High Park had been proud of that feature in the house. "The oldest surviving toilet in Toronto," he explained, his voice beaming. The bathroom had looked like a tiny wallpapered booth, the toilet like an outhouse bench.

The Flatiron guide, a chubby man with Elmer Fudd cheeks, was on a schedule, perhaps aware of the long line gathering outside. He rushed them forward to the staircase, pointing out the walk-in vault squatting on the floor. "It's from the days when the whisky baron George Gooderham raked in wheelbarrow-loads of cash from liquor sales during prohibition in the US. There used to be a safe on each floor."

Jenn caught Marta's eye. "Imagine all that money." Jenn kept her voice to a whisper.

"What is it about you and cash?" Marta said back, smiling. "I swear you should have been a banker, you like cash so much."

"More like a bank robber."

"In those days," the guide continued, "a tunnel ran underneath the building from the furnace room north to the Toronto Bank across the street. The bank is now the Pizza Pizza at the corner of Wellington and Church." Marta elbowed Jenn's arm meaningfully at the word *tunnel*. She raised her hand.

"Is the tunnel still there?"

"No, it was filled in sometime during the 1950s, but there's evidence of it in the basement."

The guide paraded them through the top floors at breakneck speed. The most interesting places—the wedge-shaped offices and the attic—were off-limits. Fingering a rope gate that blocked visitors, Marta peered with longing up the narrow spiral staircase at the top of the building. She could make out the skylight that, the guide explained, opened to the rooftop.

"Sure we can't go up—just take a peek?"

"It belongs to the dentist's office that rents the top floor," said the guide. "Maybe he's taking new clients."

"I'll check," said Marta. She felt sheepish.

The guide led them back to the lobby and ushered them outside. "Let's find that tunnel in the basement," Marta said to Jenn.

Jenn rolled her eyes like one of Marta's long-suffering ninth-graders. "You're not over that exhibit at the Grange yet, are you?" she said as she followed Marta toward the pub entrance at the back of the Flatiron Building.

Inside the pub, Marta raked her eyes across the walls in the dim dining area. They were covered with new wood panelling. Marta continued walking toward the washrooms and the kitchen.

"It's still bugging you, isn't it?"

Marta peered into the kitchen. A cook glanced at her, but turned indifferently back to whatever he was stirring. The kitchen was cluttered and hot. They couldn't get a clear look at the walls, certainly could see no signs of a tunnel. Marta took two steps forward and scanned the bits of wall visible between the frying pans and saucepans suspended from the ceiling. "Can I help you?" a waiter growled, edging past them into the kitchen.

"No, we're leaving," said Jenn. She took Marta's arm and pulled her toward the stairs.

Though the summer solstice was still a month away, the humid air hummed with the soundtrack of the city summer—pigeons, gulls, horn blasts, streetcars, construction equipment, air conditioners. So early this year, Marta thought again. As they trotted toward the subway, Marta said, "I *am* still bummed about that exhibit. The art gallery shouldn't have advertised it as historical. It was a sham." The sisters had attended the exhibit at the Grange, a two-hundred-year-old brick mansion next to the Art Gallery of Ontario. She remembered the details too clearly: the Grange claimed it had received documents from a butler who worked in the house in the mid-1800s, a butler who had witnessed a seventeen-year-old maid layering beeswax around small objects, then concealing them within the walls and under the floorboards of the house. He made a map. And then, more than one hundred and fifty years later, an excavation had exposed the objects. Marta had quivered at the oddness, thrilling to the mystery that had lived in the walls undiscovered for all that time, and to the revelation at last. She had gaped almost in rapture at the artefacts sitting in waxen shells—locks of hair, animal bones, bits of cloth, cinnamon, a rabbit skull. But three days after her visit, the *Toronto Star* printed an article about the show. "A total sham," Marta repeated now.

"Not really," Jenn said. "An art installation."

"Same thing." She edged around a bike rack and led the way through a group of tourists—seniors speaking French. A pigeon fluttered from an awning over the Shoppers Drug Mart and landed on a railing nearby. It cooed and preened its wing feathers. Something flickered inside Marta, the same flash of anticipation she had felt riding the elevator up to the ballroom a couple of hours before. There had to be some connection between the subway pigeon—the rock dove—and her own life. It had to be telling her something, inviting her to something. She certainly felt she could use some direction, some answers. But what could a pigeon mean? Or a mink—even a friendly one? The problem was that, to get answers, you needed to think, and one's trail of thought could so easily lead one into a minefield.

Jenn had been checking messages and was sliding her phone back into her handbag. She rarely went more than two hours without checking in at work, even on weekends. "I think it was clever—creating the artefacts and the history behind them. Shows more imagination than the floral watercolours that Aunt Bea makes."

"It was dishonest. Fraudulent. Even if the art gallery is free for teachers again next year, I'm not going back." Months later, just talking about it made Marta's heart sag.

THEIR LAST stop for the day was a Toronto Transit Commission ghost, a derelict subway station beneath Bay Station. Built as a turnaround so that passengers could go north-south and east-west on the same train, it had been retired after just two months of service. "Did you know this station existed?" Marta asked Jenn while they waited in a line that stretched from Bay Station far into the Cumberland Shopping Centre.

"Yes. It's where *Johnny Mnemonic* was filmed."

"Oh. I don't watch sci-fi films."

"Well, other films used this as a set too."

"I need a washroom and some food soon," Marta said.

"Want to bail on this? This line could take a while."

"No!" Marta's voice came out shrill, and Jenn laughed.

"Forgot your love of subway tunnels. Maybe there'll be a pigeon down there."

Marta glared at her sister. "Don't mock that."

The station, when they finally reached the front of the line, was unremarkable. Dingy white tiles lined the floors and walls of the platform, which ran between two tracks. Barbed wire surrounded an area on the east end of the platform filled with construction materials and debris that Marta couldn't identify. She walked to the far end of the station, trying to get away from the crowd of gawkers and the din they were creating. She sought solitude to savour what she liked: the experience of being deep beneath the city's streets, beneath an upper subway station, beneath the noise of motors and the rumbles of thunder that had started when they were still above ground. The conversations of the people around her seemed muffled; they bounced off the tile walls and disappeared along the dark, uphill tunnel that stretched in front of her.

Jenn appeared at her shoulder. "A poster over there says this station was open for Nuit Blanche a while back."

"What for?"

"You're going to love this. An art installation piece."

"Here?"

"Yes. A sound piece—a recording. Something to do with sounds below the threshold of hearing. Infrasound and tactile sound, the poster said."

"That's interesting. Sounds you feel rather than hear."

"Guess so." Jenn pulled out her cellphone. "No service down here. I suppose that's no surprise. I'll meet you at the exit. Or are you ready to go?"

"I'll join you in a minute." Marta turned to peer down the tunnel again, while Jenn edged her way back through the crowd.

"Ms. Elzinga!" The deep voice came from behind her. She turned to see the cheerful freckles of a former student, and fought for a moment to remember his name. It slipped into her mouth just as he reached her.

"Oliver Kohl. Nice to see you again." He looked about the same—lanky build, spiky hair still dyed platinum, cargo shorts, and skate shoes. She noticed the Doors Open clipboard in his hand. "You're working here?"

"Just volunteering. Employed by the city this summer. The Street Outreach Program. And I'm working on my social work degree at U of T." He paused, looking momentarily like a child presenting his mother with a newly finished drawing.

"Well, congratulations! I always knew you were smart. A summer job, university, *and* you're volunteering. I'm impressed."

He looked pleased. "Only volunteering today. I have a friend who got me this location—it's the one I wanted."

"I can see why. It's fantastic to be down here. I love subway tunnels."

"Really?"

"Yeah. I usually ride the trains in front so that I can look into the tunnel while I ride."

"Ever walked inside a tunnel?"

"No—you're not allowed, are you? I once saw someone coming out—a young guy. He looked furtive, which made me think he wasn't supposed to have been in there."

"Spoken like a teacher." Oliver's mouth stretched into a familiar tease. She had seen a lot of him during his four years at Dufferin Tech. She was green at her job, feeling even less equipped than she did now. Yet she had backed him and advised him, and she'd done her best to steer him. Behavioural problems, the teachers complained. "He's sure got high spirits," said Ian

Jones in the Phys Ed department when Marta had suggested he recruit Oliver for a sports team during a troublesome stretch of grade ten. Irrepressible—that was Oliver's main personality trait. And a lack of respect for authority, the vice-principal had made her admit after Oliver had set off the fire alarm just before the province-wide literacy test was about to begin. But here he was anyway, pursuing post-secondary education *and* giving back to the community. She felt a little vindicated for her belief in him.

"Maybe he was staying in the tunnel," Marta mused. "Do you think people live in the subway tunnels?"

"Not in Toronto. In New York they do, and maybe in Moscow, but not here. People explore them though." He was watching her face.

"How do they avoid getting hit?"

"They go at night, or, actually, very early in the morning, when the trains aren't running yet. Even then, you need to be careful because there are maintenance crews and sometimes trains going through."

"Have you done it?"

"Yeah."

"Cool," she said.

He must have heard the sincere admiration in her voice because, to her surprise, he said, "Wanna come sometime?"

"Isn't it illegal?"

"Yes. And you could get hurt. But not if you're careful. You can avoid getting caught too. The security cameras are there to look for trouble on the platform, not for people infiltrating the tunnels. You can avoid them."

"Can I think about it?"

"Sure." He smiled and began turning away. "It was nice to see you, Ms. E."

"You too. Oh, Oliver," she called to his back. "How do I get hold of you if I decide I'd like to join you?"

"You serious?"

"Are you? I mean, was your invitation serious?"

"Sure, if you want." He looked like his fourteen-year-old self again, eyes lit up with mischief.

She took out her BlackBerry. "Got an email address?"

He gave it to her, then raised his clipboard in a goodbye wave. She glimpsed a tattoo partly hidden by the short sleeve of his T-shirt, a series of tiny words in block print, and she pointed. "What—?"

He grinned again and raised the shirt sleeve obligingly. "Tolkien. My favourite author." The block letters read NOT ALL THOSE WHO WANDER ARE LOST. Above the words was a spiral design that looked Polynesian to her. Or maybe South American— she knew only European art, and the Group of Seven.

"Cool," she said. He waved again and in a moment disappeared into the thick crowd.

CHAPTER FIVE

MATT WAS RECLINING ON THE couch when Marta strolled in. In one hand he held the iPod remote, in the other, a fresh joint. His first of the day?

"Come 'ere, babe," he said, taking a drag and crushing the end on a nearby saucer.

He had stopped offering her marijuana five years ago when she got her job. "Guidance counsellors don't smoke weed," she had said.

"Singer-songwriters do."

"I'm not a singer-songwriter anymore."

"That was your decision."

She had been silent, feeling loss. Not for the pot—it loosened her control and induced paranoia. It was the singing she missed. And his interest in her when she was a performer. She regarded him now. He was not a big man: five feet, nine inches, and slight in build. So far he was slim through the middle despite several nights a week of beer drinking. He had the warm, silky eyes of a Labrador retriever; even his neutral expression was friendly. When he turned his interest to you, his gaze had the charm of a devoted dog. She'd told him that once, and he had been insulted. Well, he had never had pets as a child, didn't understand the way a dog could make you feel good just by gazing at you. That's what

Matt did, could make her feel like she was mesmerizing. She used to believe that's what he thought of her.

He held out his arms now to indicate that he wanted her to climb on top of him. First joint probably, she decided. Two—even spread over a few hours—and he was too mellow to contemplate lovemaking, certainly too mellow to follow through on any advances. She took off her sandals and slid her slim torso against his. He fiddled with the remote and changed the music. It had been The Wheat Girls; now the jazz violin of Stéphane Grappelli bounced around the room. "Afternoon in Paris." Marta's mouth curved in spite of herself, and she tilted her head to look into Matt's eyes. He smiled a lazy smile, dropped the remote, and ran his hand over her shoulder. She could feel him growing hard beneath her. "I like you in sundresses," he murmured. He undid the zipper at the back of the dress. "I like you even more out of sundresses." She nuzzled the side of his neck and breathed in the combination of scents—marijuana for sure, but underneath it the pricey aftershave she had bought him, a splurge she made because the scent made her think of riding horses through pine forests in the mountains. Probably she'd allowed herself to be bamboozled by the advertising, since the aftershave smelled—mercifully— nothing like a horse, and not much like a pine forest either. But she loved the scent, a warm, musky earth smell. And there was the scent of him, not something she had words for, but a scent that made her feel proprietary. Possessive.

Well, he would be hers for the next half-hour or more. Sex was good when he'd been smoking a little, like getting the premium pampering package at a five-star spa, or so she imagined. The drug slowed him down just enough. Long, leisurely kisses, like slow walks in an exotic territory. She would caress him while he caressed her, languid and thorough. Every bit of her from her earlobes to her baby toes would receive nuzzles, nibbles, stroking. He would be attentive to her breathing, increase speed and pressure when he sensed she wanted him to. Marta ignored the downside of the pot-smoking. So what if Matt was a little detached from her the whole time, in tune with her body but not with her soul? What woman didn't long for a slow, thorough lover? "Count your blessings," she told herself in her mother's practical voice, though she suspected her mother might not consider drugged lovemaking a sign of God's providence.

She pulled up Matt's T-shirt and ran her tongue over his chest and nipples. "Mmm," he said, the sound both contented and aroused. He ran the tips of his fingers from her shoulders down her back to her butt.

"I love you," she said, lifting her face toward his.

"Shh."

LATER, OVER a dinner of tacos that Marta made from ground beef and a boxed kit of shells, spices, and salsa, Marta told Matt about Lower Bay Station.

"You stood in line an hour to see *that*?"

"Well, it wasn't much to look at, but I like knowing what's there—underneath the ground, I mean."

"Hey, if that's how you want to spend your weekend!"

His smile was a bit patronizing, she thought. "What did *you* do today?" She heard the small barb in her tone, but he appeared not to notice.

"Worked on getting some more gigs for my bands. Hugh's Room is booked through the summer, so that's no good. There's a new club on Ossington—The Black Banjo. It's looking for acts. But it doesn't have its liquor licence yet, and I don't want my bands playing a dry room. Might as well do a church gig."

"I used to do church gigs."

"Exactly."

"Exactly what?"

"You used to do church gigs, and they were dull." Draining his beer, he caught her expression. "Not your singing—the room. Audience had sticks up their asses. No groove in the room."

She was silent. She had found the audiences polite, even appreciative. Unlike bar audiences, they stayed mostly quiet during the songs. If the church allowed a merchandise table, some audience members bought her five-song EP and asked her to sign it. Maybe it wasn't rollicking merriment, but she had enjoyed it. She had thought he had enjoyed it too.

OVERNIGHT THUNDER showers had blown away the humid air, and her trip to the Fiesta Garden Centre on Sunday afternoon was cold. Now, dressed in jeans and a jacket, she transplanted tiny flowers into patio pots: blue ageratum, lacy-leaved daisy miller, white petunias—gentle colours that would soothe the eyes on steamy afternoons in August. It had been easy to imagine those afternoons in yesterday's heat, but they seemed unlikely today.

Jenn looked on from the porch, having dropped in on her way to a dinner party. She was dropping in a lot lately, thought Marta. Ever since Marta had told her about the sightings—the mink and the pigeon. She had grabbed a beer from the fridge and the crocheted afghan from the couch, which she now draped over her head and shoulders and wrapped across her chest. "You look like the little match girl in that Hans Christian Andersen book we had when we were little," Marta said.

"She wouldn't have frozen to death if she had one of Mom's ugly afghans. But go on—your theory." She waved the fingertips sticking out of the blanket toward Marta.

Marta ripped open a bag of potting soil. She had been explaining to Jenn her belief that most major changes in life happened randomly. "Yah—they're not voluntary, or at least not fully planned—like teenage pregnancy, for instance. I think that by the time someone reaches eighteen, there will be three or four or five events that have moulded them so far," she said, pouring the soil into an empty terra cotta pot. "Events or episodes—things thrust upon them." She thought about Abdi Khalid, his life in Somalia that she knew nothing about, his move to Toronto that she knew little about. She tugged on a gardening glove and patted the soil tight. "That's the information I try to glean about my students, especially the ones at risk. What are the big things that happened to them? What's motivating them?"

"Uh huh." Jenn sipped at the Heineken, appearing unimpressed. "So what are the events that moulded you?"

Marta straightened. Should have seen this coming. "Well, you know. You were there. I'm not really one for navel gazing."

"Humour me." The indifference was gone. Jenn's eyes were a hawk's on its prey. Marta crouched to pick up a new tray of seedlings. She thought about her childhood, which made her head hurt. Reflection on the past seared, like walking into the noon sun with dilated pupils.

"C'mon," said Jenn.

"Okay, but give me a minute—I need the washroom." Marta climbed the steps, kicking off her running shoes at the door. She dawdled in the house, straightening the bed covers, returning the phone to its cradle. Was there a good reason to stay silent, or could she conjure an excuse that Jenn would accept? Jenn, in her confident, offhand manner, confided shiploads of information about her own life, sometimes more than Marta wanted. Details that Marta's students would label "over-share," like how much Jenn was missing sex since breaking off the two-year relationship with Randall, the boyfriend-who-could-not-commit. Marta passed by the fridge and poured herself a glass of wine, a cheap Chilean red that Matt had been buying lately.

"So?" said Jenn as Marta pulled the door shut and edged past her down the steps.

"Okay." She set the wine beside the porch railing. Her fingers liberated a little ageratum from the plastic seed tray, and she nudged it into the soil. "One: Dad's surgery when I was seven and you were five." A hernia, though she hadn't known what that was at the time. She glanced Jenn's way; Jenn was nodding, a crease between her eyes. "Two:"—a white geranium came next—"the camping trip when you got lost." For three hours—Jenn had slipped ahead of them on the trail and then taken a side path. There were bears in those woods. Marta packed the soil tight around the seedlings and took a cascading pink petunia from the tray. She could feel Jenn's concentration on her, but Jenn said nothing. "Three: when we moved from Lethbridge to Toronto." The trowel slipped and splattered lumps of wet dirt on the grass around the pot. Marta tried to scoop them up with her hands. Jenn set down her beer, shrugged off the afghan, and strolled over to help. "Thanks." Marta breathed in the chilly air. "Four: Aaron. Or maybe the order of those two should be switched—I'm not sure." She thought about the list. She and Aaron had dated through grade eleven. She moved to Toronto the summer after. Aaron died in the fall of grade twelve. No way to disentangle three and four.

Jenn returned to the steps, dragging her hand along the edge of the porch to remove the mud from her fingers. Marta noted what the four things she had listed had in common: the terror they generated in her. She did not say this out loud.

She pushed in the final seedlings—deep blue lobelia spilling down the edges of the pot. Give the plants a few weeks to fill in and the arrangement was going to be lovely. "Five:"—she lugged the pot to a prime spot just in front of the porch, locking eyes with Jenn and trying to keep the defensiveness from her voice—"meeting Matt."

The antidote to the fear.

HER STROKE of good fortune, or the sign of God's hand in her life—her view fluctuated with her theology—occurred at the

Mariposa Folk Festival in Orillia eight years before. She was performing; he was scouting for bands. She thought at first he was one of the festival organizers because he sounded so knowledgeable, confiding to her who was good, who was washed up, who was overrated. She herself was playing at the Acoustic Stage, which was not a stage but a tent. She'd rented a digital piano for the set, and some volunteers had helped her to set it up on the grass floor. It wobbled whenever she put pressure on the left-hand side, but she assured the volunteers that she'd make do. She apologized to the audience for the keyboard. "I don't play guitar or mandolin or the kinds of acoustic instruments you were probably expecting. It's kind of hard to travel with an upright piano." She gave a little laugh. No one else did. The Acoustic Stage sat between the Main Stage and the children's fun area. Festive bubbles floated into the tent from the giant bubble blowers outside. Occasionally a runaway toddler came in, followed by a mom or dad who scooped up the child, stayed for a few seconds, then exited. Gordon Lightfoot was playing the Main Stage; the music and the thunderous applause between songs bled into the Acoustic tent.

Marta introduced her first song. "I'm originally from Alberta"—a short woman in a patchwork top clapped—"and I wrote this song remembering the sounds of the prairie." She played the opening chords, which she had written to simulate wind. She sang the opening verse.

> The wind is a pirate who sails through the trees
> It steals my thoughts when I'm on my knees

I was praying for you
As I always do
All I hear is the rustle of leaves.

At the last line she included some high arpeggios on the piano, and
a guy at the back called out, "Yeahhh!" and clapped. She'd noticed
him when he came in. Not big, but attractively shaped. Brown hair,
a bit shaggy. He wore jeans and a grey T-shirt with PEACE MUSI-
CAL INSTRUMENTS and a drawing of a drum kit printed across it.
He stood out from all the men dressed in loud shirts, sandals, and
goofy hats.

She played the next verse, and then the bridge, getting used to
the wobble of the keyboard when she played notes more than an
octave below middle C.

I left you in a summer storm
Those smoky eyes that kept me warm
Your jealous love I did disdain
Alone I brave the wind and rain.

The man kept up his applause and approving hoots, inspiring some
audience members to smile and sway their shoulders in time to the
music. She sang the last verse with more passion than usual.

The wind is a pirate who sails through the trees
It stole my prayers when I was on my knees
Now I'm thinking of you

As I always do
Guess it's time I start praying for me
Guess it's time I start praying for me.

After the show, the man introduced himself. "Matt Bailey." He took her hand but did not shake it. "Good performance. You've got a great voice. There's something vulnerable yet powerful in it. Really great." He'd gazed at her as if she were a work of art. Up close he was even more attractive, a lean face with high cheekbones, warm brown eyes, streaky brown hair that fell in waves around his face. "Can I buy you a beer after you've packed up?"

"Oh—I don't drink beer," she said. She regretted the words. She could have sipped at a brew. The nasty taste would have been worth it to have his company.

He smiled, his eyes like melted chocolate. "An ice cream then."

"Hey, Matt!" A pot-bellied man in a baseball cap strolled over.

"Joseph! Marta, my buddy Joseph. He's playing drums for Catherine MacLellan this weekend."

Joseph shook Marta's hand, and she tried to keep her admiration and envy to herself. Maybe one day she would be playing the Main Stage with a band backing her up. "How do you two know each other?" Joseph asked.

Matt stole a look at her, eyes glinting. "We grew up together," he said, slinging an arm across Marta's shoulder. Marta stiffened, then giggled; the sound unusual to her ears. She relaxed under his arm. She hoped he would keep it there.

"Did you hear the Lightfoot concert?"

"No, I just heard Marta's show. She's an up-and-comer."

"Cool." Joseph nodded his head up and down. His glance at her looked skeptical, she thought. "Lightfoot was great. That guy's singing is stronger than ever."

"Cool." Matt waved a hand toward the food tents. "We're off to get some ice cream. Want to join us?" Matt said.

"No, I'm vegan." How did he get the pot belly on a vegan diet? Marta wondered. "I'll catch you later."

They walked past vendors selling hand-built kites, beeswax cure-alls, birdhouses, percussion instruments, hemp clothing, leather jewellery. Marta stopped to smell some handmade herbal soap, and then to admire a bracelet made of silver chain and dangling hand-blown glass beads. "That's pretty," Matt said.

"Mm-hmm." She turned away.

"Aren't you going to buy it?"

"Not today." The payment for her show wasn't enough to cover the keyboard rental, let alone the car rental for the day.

"It will look great on you. Let me buy it." He was reaching into his back pocket for his wallet.

"No." The word blasted out. "I mean, thank you—that's very sweet—but we just met, and I can't allow you to buy me a gift." She felt the embarrassment bloom in her cheeks.

Matt looked at her calmly. "Okay. This is what we're going to do. We're going to eat our ice cream very slowly—good thing it's not too hot today. By the end of the ice cream cone, you can tell me if we know each other well enough for me to buy you a tiny little thing."

She felt silly now, making a fuss over an eighteen-dollar bracelet. But you didn't let strangers buy you gifts—that message was ingrained from about the same time your mother started telling you to keep your legs closed when you were wearing a dress.

Matt led her to the organic ice cream tent. She chose ginger; he had coconut banana. They wandered to the beach and sat on a picnic table facing Lake Couchiching. The lake glistened in the afternoon sun, each glint a diamond of possibility.

She found herself chatting readily—maybe it was licking ice cream that relaxed her tongue. She told Matt about leaving Alberta for Toronto at the beginning of grade twelve. "Tough time to move," he said.

"Yeah. Everyone had friends already, and I was an oddball. A country hick in an urban school." She told him about completing a degree at the University of Toronto, commuting from her parents' home until she found a part-time job caring for a woman with advanced multiple sclerosis. "It was actually a hard way to make money. She was a control freak to begin with—she'd been a CEO somewhere before getting sick, and the disease had made her lose control. She had written out instructions for everything, even making a peanut butter sandwich."

Matt laughed, a big sound that boomed toward the lake.

"She'd yell instructions from the living room to remind me of each step, only her words were so garbled I couldn't understand."

"What did it sound like?"

"U-er uh ed urst!" Marta shrieked the words. "That meant, 'Butter the bread first.' I felt bad for her, but it was a nightmare too—spending four hours a day with someone constantly frustrated with me. Now that I think of it, she was a bully. But she paid well, and I got to move out of my parents' house in my second year and move in with two music students. That was great."

Matt fixed his eyes on her while she talked. He was sympathetic, but he saw humour in the details. Her history, as she told him, shifted subtly—it lightened; it provoked laughter. Her life story, a drama about a drab and solitary young woman, morphed into a social satire, maybe even a romantic comedy. Once Matt reached over to flip a strand of hair behind her ear. "You have gorgeous hair," he said. She had used hot rollers that morning to give it some body and wave. It bounced against her shoulders when she moved her head, different from the straight, lank way it usually fell.

"What instrument do you play?" she asked.

"Nothing. Can't read music, don't play an instrument."

She tried to hide her shock. "But you know so much . . ." She was reassessing her impression of him. A gourmand instead of a gourmet. A zealous fan rather than a musician.

"Well, I'm in the music business. I'm a manager." He sounded amused.

"Who do you manage?"

She didn't recognize the names he gave her. Later, when she looked them up online, she was relieved to find that they did exist. Small indie bands. Well, she was a small independent act too. Didn't almost everyone begin that way? But how much managing did such groups require? They played a few times a month in coffee houses on Roncesvalles, dilapidated bars on Bloor West, occasionally a College Street club. She wondered how he filled his time when he wasn't booking gigs.

He looked at his watch. "Come with me to the youth showcase?"

"Sure. Just going to use the facilities first."

"Nice name for the Johnny-on-the-spots." His eyes laughed. "I'll meet you in front of the merch tent."

The showcase was sparsely attended. Matt and Marta sat on the grass off to the side and listened to earnest youngsters singing songs they had written. The death of a grandparent was a popular theme, causing Marta to rethink her own dead-grandfather song. The other subject was, of course, unrequited love. Marta felt fondness for the kids—a strutting fifteen-year-old with Mick Jagger guitar moves, a short boy who used his long bangs to avoid eye contact with the audience, a skinny pre-teen who shook her hips like she was a Vegas superstar. While Matt commented on each act's potential or lack of it, Marta saw the vulnerability and the yearning. "Maybe I just see myself in them," she told Matt. He took her hand and stroked it.

At the end of the evening, Matt walked her to the Hyundai she'd rented. "Have a safe drive," he said. He pushed a small package into her hand.

"What's this?"

"My phone number." He kissed her cheek, waved, and ambled toward the beer tent. He was staying for an after-party. She unfolded the little bag. He'd scrawled his phone number on it. *Please call.* Inside the bag was the glass bead bracelet.

MARTA LAY on her back waiting for morning. She kept still, aware of Matt's light breathing next to her. Again, she had woken before the alarm: 6:10 AM, a full twenty minutes before her day should have begun. Enough time to register her restlessness, and to feel perplexed.

She felt like she had the summer she was fourteen, lying on her towel by a community pool in Lethbridge. Those days brimmed with promise, but by late afternoon the heat that had been so pleasant began to stifle. She remembered the irritation, the claustrophobia in spite of the breeze. Back then, the choices were easy—dive back into the water or pack up the sunscreen and towel and head home.

She could quit her job. When she had popped into a grade nine classroom last Friday searching for one of the English teachers, she read the day's journal topic on the board. *Imagine that you skipped school today. Where would you go? What would you do?* She found herself fantasizing about a chilly morning walk in High Park. A latte and the *Globe and Mail* at The Starving Artist on Lansdowne. She heard Jenn's voice in her head. "How would you pay your rent? How long before you'd be bored and aimless?"

Maybe it was time to have a baby—that notion had visited her with some frequency lately. She was thirty, a good age to start a family. But was it right to bring a child into a marriage that, well, had its problems? Matt wasn't opposed to having kids, but he hadn't suggested she stop taking the pill either.

Maybe she just needed a new hobby. Yoga. It was designed to cure restlessness. Well, stress, but that was probably the same thing. Or stained glass. There was a studio a couple of blocks away that offered workshops. She could make little sun-catchers. Get really good and design a full window forest scene à la Group of Seven.

The buzz of her alarm was a relief. She heaved herself up and gratefully began the routine of the day.

WHEN SHE arrived home that night, Matt was out. He texted her at 6:00 PM: Meeting with a new singer. Won't be home for dinner. XO. Marta made Cup-a-Soup and toast with spiced Gouda. She added some mini carrots to her plate and took it to the desk in the corner of the living room. She played solitaire on the computer. She googled *mink Toronto*, which produced links to the Mink Nightclub, as well as several places to buy mink coats. She tried Google Images, which produced photos of the Mink Nightclub and of people at the Mink Nightclub, but no minks. She erased the *Toronto* in the search window and added *screensaver*. Rows of pictures popped up, and she scrolled through them until she found a mink that looked like hers. A sleek and friendly mink, headed away but looking back at the camera. She set the photo as the desktop wallpaper and noted the satisfaction this act brought her.

Marta looked at the clock. Only 7:00 PM. She surveyed the narrow room. The piano, a graceless old clunker, prevented any hope of the feng shui that her friend Lily encouraged her to aim for in the house. It jutted almost halfway into the room from the southern wall. iPod speakers and a small flatscreen TV decorated its top. The faux leather sofa they'd bought at the Brick with wedding money six years ago sagged against the northern wall, and the computer desk sat awkwardly in the corner, like a time-out chair. Mismatched artwork—a drooping peony painted by Aunt Bea and a laminated poster advertising the first Lilith Fair—hung on the dark beige walls. The landlord had refused to let them change the paint colour, even when Marta offered to repaint the walls when they left. Marta gazed outside. The front window was drafty, but a cheerful stained glass pane decorated the top of it, and at this hour sleepy sunrays made the glass glow with red and amber light. Across the street Mrs. Pereira was hosing down her paved front yard and her wrought-iron railings. Marta reminded herself to water her patio pots before she left for school in the morning. But what now?

She could check email. She got up and retrieved her BlackBerry from her purse, wanting to keep the mink in view on the desktop computer. Her mother had forwarded photos of her cousin Sandra's new twins, and Lily wondered if she wanted to go to the art gallery on the weekend. She replied to Lily: I'll pass on the art gallery, but maybe we could go to the museum? She wasn't all that interested in the current exhibit at the ROM, something about water, she thought, but Lily's nursing shifts sometimes made it difficult for the two of them to get together—best to say yes when Lily was available. She deleted some junk mail and the photos of the babies. Then, time hanging on her like a sloth, she scrolled through her contacts.

She paused at Oliver Kohl's email address. She remembered the words on his arm: NOT ALL THOSE WHO WANDER ARE LOST. She thought of the tunnels, the long and beckoning passageways. If she got caught, she could lose her job. The school board would not overlook a criminal charge, even if it was just for trespassing. She noticed her toes squirming up and down, and relaxed her foot.

She typed, telling herself she could delete the message without sending it. Or write a different one.

> Hi, Oliver,
> If you're okay with having me tag along, I would like to join you for the exploration you were telling me about. If you've changed your mind, that's okay too.

She signed it *Marta* and put *Ms. E* in parentheses after the *Marta*, just in case he didn't recognize her first name. Her finger twitched and jiggled over the Send key. She recalled her restlessness that morning and felt it return, the dissatisfaction, the yearning. She longed for a clearer sense of purpose. She thought of praying, but since the pigeon sighting two weeks before, God had seemed remote. She knew he had infinite energy, and she could appeal to him to come closer. But she didn't want to impose, didn't want to be troublesome or needy. She thought of one of her students, Tiffany Ng, who found a reason to pop into Marta's office almost daily, a little waif of a girl, fourteen years old with the emotional needs of an eight-year-old. No. God, she hypothesized, had paid her enough attention for the time being, and she should let him attend to more serious problems. Mercedes Lopez, for instance, and dozens more like her at Dufferin Tech alone. And then there was the rest of the world.

She turned back to the computer and observed the mink. She thought its beady eyes conveyed approval, even encouragement. She let her fingers dance. *Eeny, meeny, miny, mo.* Yes. She pressed Send.

PART TWO

OTHER PLACES

There are other places
Which also are the world's end, some at the sea
  jaws,
Or over a dark lake, in a desert or a city—
                    —T.S. Eliot, "Little Gidding"

CHAPTER SIX

MARTA NURSED INDECISION FOR A week after Oliver suggested visiting a storm drain. "You said you're worried about getting caught. We're safer in a drainpipe than in a subway tunnel."

"Won't it be disgusting down there?" she emailed back after another early morning awakening, creeping out of bed before six to fret and wait for sunrise in the living room.

"It's not a sewer—just storm water. You'd wear rain pants and rubber boots. It's cool—trust me." And reasons to join him darted kaleidoscopelike through her mind: the tunnels, the dove, the mink, the tattoo. She avoided scrutiny of her decision, but noted how it buoyed her mood in the days between Oliver's invitation and their meeting.

Matt glanced up from his calendar as she slid into the kitchen with her purse and the large tote bag that she used for carrying home reports and paperwork. This evening it held rubber boots and rain gear. "Got a school thing tonight?"

"Kind of—getting together with a former student."

"Have fun," said Matt, turning back to the calendar. Marta noticed it looked emptier than usual, only five gigs booked for June.

"I will. Are you getting your bands into festivals this summer?"

Matt ran a hand through his hair. It was dishevelled, an appealing tangle of waves. "Mariposa rejected The Wheat Girls—I don't know why. They've got lots of other acts that aren't as good." He sounded peevish as he tapped the pen on the calendar. He raised his head. "I think Nancy Jacota—that singer who just signed with me—will play at Hillside. Do you want to go?"

Marta was surprised. She shifted her tote bag behind her arm. "Sure. For the weekend or the day?"

"Let me see if I can score us festival passes. Maybe we can camp for the weekend."

"That would be nice." Marta's voice caught a little, she was so pleased.

"Okay if Nancy comes with us? She might not want to camp, but I'm sure she'd like a ride up there and would want to hang with me at the festival."

Marta let the tote slide forward, heedless of the way it slipped open and revealed the boots. "Okay." She strode toward the door. "See you later." She shut the door firmly, the thud like a gavel pronouncing a decision.

SHE MET Oliver near Mt. Pleasant and Roxborough, parking beside a row of houses far more spacious and elegant than her own. Oliver had emailed a link to information about the drain underneath this neighbourhood, but, as she gazed at the freshly paved road, the smooth driveways, and the clipped lawns around her, the existence of a subterranean world seemed as unlikely as unicorns or hobbits. Eyes darting to the windows perched high on the ridge across the street, she pulled her rain pants over her jeans and switched her leather flats for rain boots. She locked the car and scurried to the manicured lawn of a city park, swinging her arms in an effort to look nonchalant. Oliver was waiting for her, a short distance across the park. He was dressed to tunnel: a dark, tattered raincoat, black rubber boots, two miner's headlamps dangling from his hand. Still looked like a kid, she noted, though the thin, adolescent body was filling out; his shoulders were broader. The freckled face framed by the platinum tufts was still poster-boy cute, but maybe the expressions were less swaggering, more knowing. His eyes were the same, sea-coloured and brimming with anticipation. She remembered thinking one day as he had bounced into her office that he brought his own weather system with him, a system both sunnier and more tumultuous than the actual weather.

He grinned now as he watched her approach. She moved a hand up in a sort-of salute, wondering if she looked like a soldier with her marching gait and the stiff arm movements. Ah, well. She smiled in his direction, a genuine smile, not the sort she pasted on her face so often lately. The nice thing about being a teacher, she thought as she drew up beside him, was that you weren't really expected to be cool. The kids were cool, and teachers were nerdy, and the best you could hope for was fond amusement. That was why Oliver was taking her along, she was sure.

"You're going to love it," he said by way of greeting. "This way." He jerked his thumb and swung his head eastward.

"Great."

She followed him to the edge of the lawn, along a pathway through a narrow strip of woods. Like a trail guide, he moved branches aside, pointed out uneven ground. But when they reached the manhole cover, he asked for Marta's help. "It's heavy." She could hear the water below it, a rushing sound like a bathtub tap on full. "The water drops here—you're hearing an underground waterfall. Come on, you'll see it in a sec." She bent down and tugged with Oliver, lifting and pulling at the same time, shifting the metal onto the dirt with a thump.

If she had gone home at that point, Marta thought, she would already have felt some satisfaction. The same secret joy she had felt on the day she and Jenn had eluded their parents' supervision during a lazy afternoon at Indian Battle Park in Lethbridge and explored the coulees near the High Level Bridge. They poked around in the prairie grass, chased grasshoppers, picked bouquets of asters, black-eyed Susans, and goldenrod. They sang Sunday school songs at the top of their voices, while the ever-present wind snatched the sound away before it could even begin to travel across the flat expanses between the coulees. They had stared up at the glittering bridge that soared across the Oldman River valley—the highest and longest railway bridge of its kind in the world, they'd learned in school—and made a pact to cross it when they were teenagers. "We'll go to jail," Jenn said, eyes aglow. She was maybe seven at the time. "We'll come *really* early in the morning, before *anyone* is up," said Marta. "What if a train comes?" Jenn asked. "There are barrels of water up there for the firefighters. You just jump inside. But you have to keep your head down, or the train will cut it off." Jenn looked impressed. Together they had gawped at the colossal steel legs of the bridge, giant versions of the beaters their mom unplugged from the electric mixer and let them lick. They shook hands to seal the plan, their first-ever serious handshaking. Marta remembered fear and anticipation dancing through her like a fireworks sparkler. The plan made her tingle with life. And with a need to pee.

She skimmed the thin woods around her now for onlookers— the path was just a couple of metres away—then donned the vinyl raincoat she had tied around her waist. The evening was dust-dry, the sun still blazing in the June sky. Oliver pulled on his headlamp and shimmied into the manhole, calling up instructions as he disappeared. "When you get to the bottom, step to the right. You'll be in a few inches of water, but it won't be over your boots."

Marta peered around her again, senses working like a bloodhound's nose. She noted the stillness in the air, the absence of breeze on her face, the silence of the fresh June leaves around her. The loudest sound was the water, but there was also birdsong— she identified a crow, some sparrows, what sounded like a thrush. Far off, a dog barked, the high-pitched frenzy of a Pomeranian or a chihuahua. Marta, heart sputtering, contemplated the metal ladder plunging into darkness, studied it the way a child gazes at the water from a lofty diving board. The vinyl rain gear was asphyxiating her; the sun felt oppressive. She stepped forward, placed her foot on the third rung down, stooped, and began to descend, one foot, the other foot, one hand, the other hand. The rungs were cool, round steel, the ladder like those pressed against the silos she knew back in Lethbridge, straight metal bars set between straight metal poles. She curled her fingers all the way around each rung, the way she had when she climbed the silo on her friend Allie's farm more than a decade before. Only then they had climbed up, not down—up for a better view of the earth on which they'd been standing. This trip was like Alice's into Wonderland, down a rabbit hole, a worm hole. She counted rungs. Seven, eight. The pocket of her raincoat, bulging with wallet, keys, cellphone, and an extra flashlight, caught for a moment, and she twisted to free it, observing that next time she needed to travel less encumbered. Thirteen, fourteen. With each step, the temperature dropped. The air above the ground was in the mid-twenties. Oliver told her that the tunnels were a consistent fifteen degrees, whatever the time of year or the temperature above ground.

The water was a cacophony of white noise at the bottom, so loud that Oliver had to lean toward her and shout to be heard. She could feel her rubber boots and her feet inside them cool as she stood in the ankle-deep water that coursed down the gentle slope of the drain. She was standing in a round pipe just under four metres in diameter. The walls were made of large concrete panels. Her headlamp shone on some graffiti—the initials C.J.K., she thought, on one of the walls, making her wonder who else came down here. When she swung her head—and thereby her headlamp—to the left, she could make out a platform a ways above them. It was lightly littered with old leaves and garbage—shredded bits of plastic bag. The smell was earthy—like potatoes, or the root cellar on Aaron's farm.

"You okay?"

"Yes."

"Stay here a sec. I'm going to see if we can get to the outfall."

"The outfall?" She spoke with the volume she used in music clubs thick with bass and drums.

"Where this water flows into Yellow Creek. It's down there. I'll just be a sec."

He sloshed away from her, curving around a gentle corner. She stood alone in the roar of water, her headlamp illuminating a featureless expanse of concrete wall.

MARTA COULD count on one hand the number of times she had cried since Aaron's death. This had troubled her at first, but she rationalized that outward expressions of grief were just not in her nature. "I feel sad from time to time, but I don't seem to need to cry about it" was how she explained it to Jenn, whose eyebrows had popped up like toast.

When she was twelve, the year Aaron moved to Lethbridge, the church council had installed a signboard in front of the Covenant Christian Reformed Church. Along with her father's name, *Reverend Jacob Elzinga*, and the schedule of church services, the board offered a Bible verse or Christian aphorism for the local community to reflect on. These changed monthly, and Marta knew from her dad's frustrated tone when he updated her mother on the church council meetings that they were the subject of a great deal of discussion. Her dad prevailed against the council when they proposed *Prepare to meet thy maker* as the February text, arguing that, with the blind intersection just down the hill from the church, passersby might find the words ominous or, at the very least, in bad taste. *Thankfulness leaves no room for discouragement* was the council members' replacement. Her dad called it "the lesser of two evils." His tone was sour as pickled herring. "I live in gratitude to

God," Marta heard him tell her mother, "but I still have room for discouragement. Lots of room."

"Maybe you just have more interior space than most people," said Marta's mom. Marta, stacking the dishwasher while her parents talked at the table, pictured the inside of his head as a huge house with big, drafty rooms. She thought her own head had similar space.

"Yeah. That's not funny. I'm serious about this. I don't like slapping people on the wrist for feeling bad. For feeling doubt or sorrow or discouragement. Making them think they're not Christian enough if they're not happy-clappy all the time. In fact"—his voice rose like he was announcing the solution to a math problem—"I'm going to preach about that next week."

"What text will you use?" Her mother's questions were practical. She didn't experience the same heights and depths that Marta's father seemed to. Perhaps they were well matched, although, at twelve, Marta had already noted her mother's failure to take her dad's tribulations as seriously as Marta thought they deserved to be.

"I'll use the beatitude. Matthew 5. 'Blessed are those who mourn.'" He sounded pleased.

Despite her dad's self-proclaimed belief in sorrow, he had had a hard time with Marta's reaction to Aaron's death five years later. The first month he hugged her often. "Your feelings will lighten with time. Don't blame yourself—you are not responsible." But months later, in December, the bleakness still hung on her like mourning clothes, and she heard her parents talking about her, their voices twisting like hands wringing in worry.

Her dad tried music next. Beethoven, mostly. "Beethoven," he told her, "knew how much his listeners could handle—how much tension, how much sorrow, how much tragedy. Just when you can't take it anymore, he lightens the mood." He showed her, as they listened to the second movement of Symphony No. 7 together. "God's like that too." He put his hand over hers. "He doesn't give you more than you can bear. 'Weeping may endure for the night, but joy comes in the morning.'"

That was not Marta's experience. Days were joyless, and nights were spent with eyes open and dry.

So Marta's reaction to being underground took her by surprise. Not exhilaration, apprehension, or wonder. Weeks later, when she confessed to Jenn about the exploration, she would tell her, "You know that feeling you get in the top of your nose when you're going to cry—that's how I felt most of the time when I was underground."

"FOLLOW ME—you'll like this." Oliver motioned toward the curve in the tunnel.

She splashed her way toward him, then noticed his method of walking and followed suit. She opened up her stance and placed her feet just above the water on the curving sides of the pipe. She took short steps with legs apart, knees soft, as if she were walking down the aisle of a swaying train. Stay out of the ditch, she imagined her mother saying.

As she moved around the bend, she was surprised to see daylight. Oliver was standing in front of a grille, a circular gate several metres in diameter with heavy bars running horizontally and vertically. She sloshed toward it. Beyond the grille she could see trees and shrubs—sumac and bush honeysuckle and the invasive dog-strangling-vine. It was quieter here, away from the falling water nearer the manhole, and warmer too. She caught up to Oliver.

"What's this?"

"The outfall. We entered the tunnel near the top of the ravine, and now we're in the side of the hill, looking out. See?" He pointed forward. The water flowed through the bars down a short slope to a flat bed about five metres long on which she counted eleven concrete blocks and a row of what looked like parking curbs, six of them set side by side. "Those blocks are called churn blocks—they slow the water down during a storm. From here, it rolls down a short drop into the creek."

The creek, Marta knew, flowed southeast to join the Don River. She felt oriented again, pictured the manhole on top of the hill behind them. She peered at the flat stone walls of the creek close to the outfall, obviously manmade, and later decorated with swirling graffiti tags in blue, green, and red. Farther downstream more large rocks jutted out of the water. Just past the barriers a tree had grown sideways over the creek—Marta squinted through the sunlight at the bright yellow-green of its June foliage. Today, the water coursed smoothly past the obstacles, but it was not hard to imagine storm water spewing out of the pipe, accelerating down the slope, the collisions with the barriers angering it into a churning spray.

"Pretty, eh?" Oliver said. She turned to look at the woods on the edge of the creek, at the Norway maples, fresh green goldenrod, a willow. She shrugged and gave a half-smile. The fresh colour was appealing but familiar. She wanted to explore the subterranean world behind her.

She looked down at the water they stood in, now illuminated by sunlight. Marta had been prepared for filth, but, as Oliver had claimed, the water was only slightly greyish, like dishwater or ditch water. "Mostly rain," Oliver said when she commented on the lack of smell.

"What if it rains while we're down here?"

"We wouldn't be down here if there was rain in the forecast. I've never seen it, but I've heard that the stream can change to a torrent in just a few minutes."

Marta imagined again the water roaring, this time at them, rising waist-high, or neck-high, maybe filling the entire tunnel, pinning them against the grille. The thought was frightening but exhilarating too. She looked through the bars. The vantage point made it look like the world was behind bars, like the world was in jail and she had come to visit. "Let's go back into the tunnel," she said.

"We're still in the tunnel. Not getting out this way either." Oliver grinned and pointed at the grille, its openings too small for even a toddler to wiggle through.

"I mean, let's go back. I want to be under the ground, not in daylight."

"Okay. I'll show you the waterfall." He headed back toward the manhole, and she followed him into the darkness. Her headlamp needed adjusting—she should have done it while she was in daylight. It kept drifting downward over her eyes. She fiddled with the strap at the back, while at the same time watching her step on the slippery surface. The sound increased as they drew near the waterfall. The description she'd read said this drainpipe included several waterfall chambers. The one they were hearing was a large structure that split the water flow in two a ways above them, forcing it to run into a pair of side-by-side drops of about four and a half metres to the level they were at, about fifteen metres underground. Here there were also large concrete churn blocks to slow the water as it fell. She could just make out a ladder that climbed to the catwalk at the top of the waterfall. "Careful," Oliver said. He had to yell to be heard again. He put out his arm to stop her and pointed his flashlight toward the ground. "See that?"

Marta wasn't sure what there was to see. The water looked slightly darker than the water in which they were standing.

"It's a pit underneath the fall. I don't know how deep it goes, but you don't want to walk there. It's called a plunge pool." Marta took a step back.

They climbed the ladder near the falls, sidestepping to get onto it, since it descended down underneath the water into the pit. Marta held on tight as she followed Oliver up the steps. Water from his boots dripped onto her bare hands. She regretted leaving on her rings, especially the little diamond she and Matt had chosen from an antique market when they got engaged. She hoped she had sanitary wipes in the car.

The platform gave them a head-on view of the falls. Oliver shone his flashlight forward. Marta stood still. She had never seen or heard anything quite like it. The vertical channel was narrow, all straight angles, built of cement. Two small holes in the cement far above them allowed water to surge out in two mighty, rushing torrents. The subterranean waterfalls roared in the dark.

Her eyes stung, and her nose tingled.

AS SHE climbed, she noticed the temperature rise and the sound of the water recede. The sun was still shining, a bright glow at the manhole opening. At the top, the water sounded again like the bathtub tap, filling the tub in a nearby room. Oliver, already out of the manhole, shushed her as she grasped the top rung, putting a finger to his lips. "Someone coming," he said. They stayed still while an elderly couple walked along the path just a few metres away through the trees.

"That was really great," said Marta as she took off her raincoat.

"I'm meeting my buddy now." Oliver sounded a bit awkward, as if he wasn't sure how to end their encounter. "See that path?" He pointed south. "It runs right above the storm sewer."

Marta liked that, the fact that she could now walk along a pathway and picture what lay beneath. She wondered if there had been pedestrians strolling above them while she and Oliver were exploring, ambling along oblivious to the tunnel and the water underneath. "I'm going to explore the area before I go home. Maybe look at the outfall from the outside. Thanks again," she said. She handed him the flashlight and strode away before his discomfort rubbed off on her. She glanced at her watch. Only an hour had passed. She was walking toward the outfall, but, really, she wanted to go back underground, not see the tunnel from the daylight side of the grille.

She waited till she was sure Oliver would be gone, then meandered to her car. She shed the rain pants, changed to shoes, and scrubbed at her hands with a napkin from the glove compartment before she drove away.

CHAPTER SEVEN

THE SCHOOL YEAR ENDED IN its usual fizzle in the guidance department. Some of Marta's at-risk students had passed enough courses to graduate, drifting out of the school and into someone else's trouble heap—their family's, a college's, an unsuspecting employer's. Her younger students would return in the fall, most likely with their problems unaddressed, left to fester through the summer months. Though she thought of herself as less jaded than the older counsellors in her department, Marta had learned to expect little from most of the families. She would clutch the phone, hand perspiring from the weight of the news she was bearing—*your child has bulimia / has an addiction / is pregnant.* Without kids of her own, it was hard to know how she would react to news of this magnitude. She thought that sort of phone call would be—should be—like receiving news that your identity had been stolen. But parents reacted as if she were pestering them, a collection agency calling about another unpaid bill.

So summer was, partly, a relief. Unless there was a concrete reason to call Children's Aid or the police, Marta had no mandate to take responsibility after the June exams. No way to contact the students she had sent on to specialists, to see how they were coping, whether or not they were recovering. It was liberating to be cut off but anxiety-producing too. Three years before, one of her students had died on the 401 in a crash with a tractor-trailer. She hadn't known till she returned to school the last week of August. The girl had been cremated; there wasn't even a grave to visit.

On the professional development day after the students had left for the summer, Marta cleaned off her desk, turned to her computer, and opened a document with copy for the guidance department website, which the principal had assigned her to proofread before she left. Her eyes skimmed the predictable phrases—"Student Services will aid students with the transition to high school . . . can help them with social and emotional issues . . . will guide them with college, university, and career plans." It was the statement in large block letters under a photo of two girls engrossed in their math textbooks that gave her pause: THE GUIDANCE COUNSELLORS AT DUFFERIN TECHNICAL SECONDARY SCHOOL ARE COMMITTED TO HELPING YOUR TEENAGER MAKE EXCELLENT LIFE CHOICES. "Excellent." She stared at the word. Most of their students were the products of working-class homes, more than half of them from first-generation immigrant parents working long hours to survive. Their choices were small. Not insignificant, but small. And much of the time, things just happened to them. *Excellent* choices belonged to wealthier children. To luckier children.

Here it was again, her own past standing in her way like a dust cloud. She did want her students to make good life choices. But she knew how choice could elude you. Take herself, for instance. Wrenched from the prairie to Toronto, a city that was foreign despite how well she appeared to blend in, a white, middle-class girl. But, coping with the disaster that was Aaron's death, she felt like an alien, numb and disconnected from her pop-culture-loving, brand-name-obsessed grade twelve classmates. Maybe it would have been easier if she had been an immigrant from Asia. People in grade twelve were kinder to the Sri Lankan girl being sponsored by the local Christian Reformed Church, more inclusive of her, than they were to Marta.

Marta changed the "excellent" to "the best possible" and trotted to the main office to leave the document with the principal's secretary.

When she got home, perspiring from the walk through humid air, lugging a briefcase stuffed with detritus from her desk, she retrieved the mail from the tin box on the porch. A pizza flyer, an offer of ROOF REPARS FREE ESTIMIT, and a brown manila envelope from the Lethbridge Christian Reformed Church. Forehead furrowed, Marta dropped the junk mail into the recycling bin beside the porch and tore open the envelope. She pulled out a white business envelope addressed to her, c/o Lethbridge Christian Reformed Church. It was her handwriting; she recognized it immediately. Except it was not her handwriting anymore. The writing was in purple ink, with loopy *e*'s and little circles instead of dots over the *i*'s. It looked a bit silly. Or hopeful, maybe. She felt a little disoriented and pressed her hand against the cool brick wall of the house.

She knew what the envelope contained: the letter Mr. Maas, her grade eleven social studies teacher, had his students write to themselves at the end of grade eleven. Just before she moved to Toronto.

Lowering herself into the stained resin chair on the porch, she twiddled the letter in her fingers. Her eyes found the planters, and she noted with satisfaction the way the seedlings were filling in and spilling over the edges, a profusion of green, blue, and white. She linked her toe through the wrought iron of the porch railing, observing the peeling paint. Maybe she would touch it up this summer.

"Next year will be busy," Mr. Maas had said. "Starting in the fall, all the talk will be about what universities, colleges, or jobs you're applying to and where you're off to next. Before that all starts, I want you to reflect. Write a letter to yourself, telling yourself your hopes and dreams. Write about the person you want to be in your adult life. What kind of person do you want to marry? What are your career goals? And who do you want to be? Be honest. Be daring. No one will read this except you. Address the envelope care of your parents or someone who will know where you will be thirteen years from now."

"Unlucky number," someone had shouted. Paul Mercer, probably. He liked a lot of air time.

"No such thing," Mr. Maas had replied. "God is the god of all numbers." Marta remembered that.

"I won't read the letters," Mr. Maas told them. "I'll keep them for thirteen years after you graduate, then I'll mail them."

Marta rose, unlocked the door, and wrenched it open. She slid the letter into her tote bag with the rest of the accumulated litter of the year and deposited it in the hall closet. No need to read it—the letter would contain the hopeful, dreamy musings of someone with loopy handwriting who was as foreign to her now as that faraway classroom in which she wrote it.

THE HILLSIDE Festival came during a July weekend with rain in the forecast, lots of rain. Soggy camping and Nancy Jacota. But how else would she pass the time? Though the online summer course she had signed up for gave her lots of reading and writing to do during the weekdays, plenty of free hours remained. Oliver had emailed about another expedition, but nothing specific had been arranged.

Nancy Jacota moved like a Pilates instructor, with the core strength of a dancer but not the grace. She had milkmaid looks, wavy, straw-coloured hair pulled back in a sort of halo on the top of her head. Big, round breasts atop a chiselled torso. What was odd about her was the lack of expression. Her mouth rarely changed position. The perfect lips moved ever so slightly to form polite words. Marta would have thought it was her own effect on Nancy, would have taken it personally, had she not heard Nancy perform at the Manulife Indigo a few weeks before and seen the same thing. How could someone sing so clearly and with enough volume without opening her mouth?

Beauty was nothing Marta had ever yearned for. She looked good enough; that was her self-image through high school. A bit serious, those eyes of hers, and her hair a bit lank. Her face was unremarkable, but it had pleasant, even features. Great looks faded. What if attractiveness was what you were blessed with, if that was the gift God gave you? It would begin to fade just a few years after you had learned its value. So different from other gifts, most of which increased with age and practice. Mathematicians, for instance, didn't have to cope with their abilities starting to diminish in their thirties, the numbers they loved turning against them as they hurtled through middle age. Pianists could depend on their skills lasting for decades, their fingers nimble and ears attuned as long as they put time and effort into practising. No, beauty was not a gift to yearn for.

Nancy's attractiveness was unsettling though. Marta did not give up the front seat for the guest, as she sometimes did when Matt offered a ride to a client.

Matt seemed subdued. If they were alone, she would have asked him what was wrong. Maybe there would be a chance in their tent, later tonight. Or tomorrow night. Festivals were strange that way—you could spend hours—a couple of days—with your companion without talking about anything except the music, the weather, and the food.

"How's your course?" he said as they turned off the 401 and headed north toward Guelph.

"Fine. A bit strange to be doing it online. Trying to get a sense of who people are from what they write. A lot of them seem younger than me. Full of optimism. They think they're going to change the world."

"What are you taking?" asked Nancy.

"Career Guidance for At-risk Students." Marta's voice came out weary.

"Sounds useful." Nancy's voice was expressionless.

"Marta's work *is* useful." Matt sounded proud. Surprise stiffened Marta's face for a moment before pleasure suffused her. "She cares about the kids she works with."

"That's cool," said Nancy, her tone utterly flat. "Wish I had a decent guidance counsellor when I was in high school. All I remember about mine was that he stared at my tits while he had me fill out course selection forms." Marta watched Matt's eyes flicker to the rear-view mirror.

"I try," said Marta. "Sometimes there's not much I can do." She rolled her eyes in Matt's direction. He appeared not to notice.

AT THE Lake Stage, listening to a local act she'd never heard of, Marta had a brainstorm.

The trio was unremarkable in every way, from the soprano's tendency to sing sharp, to their lack of mastery over their instruments, to their stage banter and their confessional songs. Even their outfits were drab—the gaunt guitar player in jeans and brown wool, the two women in '50s-style dresses with high necklines and pleated waists that did not flatter their hips. It was the third song. Marta could hardly hear it through the din of conversation around her. The audience had packed into the tent because it was one of the few dry spaces to wait out the rain. The Main Stage was shut down, the field a muddy mess. The guitar player—Marta hadn't caught his name—sang the lead vocals, a relief from the soprano who had been leading. "It'll only get better," she thought she heard. The tune was in a minor key, undercutting the hopeful lyric. "It has to get better. It's just stormy weather. It'll only get better soon." The tune and lyrics were humdrum; yet the song tugged at her. Maybe it was the course she was taking, the thought of all the people so young and already hopeless. When she let herself think about the misery of many of her students, she felt paralyzed. Or maybe it was Aaron. Maybe this was a song that Aaron could have written if he had been a songwriter. He had written to her twice after she moved to Toronto. The first email was a paragraph long. It began: "You probably don't care, but so far summer sucks. It's drier than ever, and every day I have to install pipes for the new irrigation system in our sunflower fields. I hate sunflowers. I miss you." She hadn't replied. Breaking up with him had been difficult, like explaining the math homework to a dim classmate. She had delivered her prepared speech to him twice: "I'm a little young to stay attached to someone and have a long-distance relationship at my age. It's better if we get to know other people." When he failed to understand, or at least to accept, she got much blunter than she had planned. "I-AM-BREAKING-UP-WITH-YOU." His second email, in late August, was hostile. "Everything sucks. Even you." She had deleted the email and emptied the virtual trash bin.

What had he actually been thinking? She thought of the letter she'd received a couple of weeks ago. Her letter, written to herself. But they'd all written to themselves, Aaron too. It was a week or two after they'd broken up, so they'd never talked about what they put in their letters. She felt a longing to know.

This was her brainstorm: she would read Aaron's letter. It could hold some answers.

She needed a computer with Internet. She needed to find Mr. Maas's address. Would he be retired now? Did he still live in Lethbridge? She was sure she could find him—or if she couldn't, her dad could locate him through his church contacts. The Dutch

Christian Reformed community might blend in well enough with mainstream culture that their differences were invisible, but in reality they were as insular as the other ethnic groups that settled in Canada.

If only she weren't stuck in the rain at the Guelph Lake Conservation Area listening to bad music.

She wondered whether or not Mr. Maas had kept the letter—did he pull it out when Aaron died and destroy it? Maybe he gave it to Aaron's parents. But the letter wasn't there in the funeral home. She pictured the cheerless display of Aaron's possessions. His parents, or someone, had put together an exhibit of photographs of Aaron and some of his personal effects—sketches he'd drawn: the barn, a face she didn't recognize. And there was schoolwork too. His parents must have been given the contents of his locker. Marta imagined Mr. Vandenakker, the young caretaker who was usually sneaking a smoke behind the school, prying off the lock and emptying the contents into a garbage bag. And, later, Aaron's parents going through it, rifling the pages of his math text, the fresh notebooks with subject labels but little else. It was only the second week of September. *Why Study Biology?* was the heading of the first note. He had dutifully copied down the first sentences from the teacher's note on the board: *We strive to understand the wonders of God's creation. We see God as the creator and sustainer of our world and study the ways in which He has designed the planet and its creatures to proclaim His glory. At the same time, we will examine how the fall into sin impacted creation, causing creation to groan, sending disease and trouble into the world.* Marta's parents had forbidden her from taking biology at

Calvin Christian High School. The school had hired a man from the conservative Netherlands Reformed community, who, Marta's father predicted, was going to "make it his mission to turn the lot of you into creationists, all evidence to the contrary." Marta often thought that, if her father's congregation discovered his true beliefs on a number of controversial topics, they'd try to defrock him.

After the note, Aaron had apparently tuned out. There was a sketch of some object—a microscope?—crossed out with a violent pen stroke. And then came empty pages blaring the sudden, too-early end of his life. Next to the notebooks on the funeral home table lay his pencil case, with graffiti mostly written by others. *Hi Aaron, Whatcha doin? Dude!* She'd noted that the tiny noose that had been attached to the zipper last May and June was gone. She remembered reaching for his English notebook, both hoping and dreading that maybe there were journals, a piece of creative writing that would illuminate his interior life. She was ashamed that she felt relief at finding only a note on pronouns and, on the second page, a list of books for independent study. A thin line surrounded *Funny Boy* by Shyam Selvadurai. She remembered how peculiar it had seemed to her that he circled a title of a book, as if he had been intending to read it.

Marta rose. The soprano was singing again, a cappella this time, with the alto gamely trying to match harmonies to the meandering pitch of her bandmate. Lifting her raincoat hood over her head, Marta left the tent and traipsed through drizzle toward the beer tent to look for Matt and Nancy. She would have to pursue Aaron's letter another time. After the weekend, anyway. She tried not to get her hopes up. The class had been skeptical about the assignment. She remembered the murmurs as they pulled out paper and pens—would Mr. Maas really refrain from reading the letters, would he actually remember to send them thirteen years later? It was unlikely Aaron had confided anything significant in his letter. She thought *she* hadn't. Though her letter was still stowed unopened in her closet, she remembered it being breezy and light. Or maybe that was her authentic self back then—breezy and light. It was hard to know.

"Marta!" The voice came from a figure skipping toward her in a long purple rain poncho and flowered boots. She was carrying what looked like a guitar case wrapped tightly in a yellow garbage bag. "Marta! It's me, Joelle! Remember, we met at Mariposa?"

"Joelle. Didn't recognize you for a sec. Hey, what's up?"

"Things are great." Joelle shifted the guitar case to her other hand. "We've been touring all over the place lately. Still singing! Have a pretty good following in Australia of all places—we've toured there every year for the last four years. What about you? Are you performing this weekend?"

"Uh—no. I'm a teacher now. A guidance counsellor."

"Oh." Marta could feel Joelle's interest cool. "That's great. Are you still with—sorry, I don't remember his name. The manager."

"Matt. Yes. He's here somewhere." Marta glanced toward the beer tent, its yellow-striped awning visible beyond a stand of spruce trees.

"Well, say hi to him. Come to our show later if the rain stops. Main Stage at five o'clock."

"Definitely." Marta let the smile she had mustered fade as Joelle waved and headed toward the performer tent. A crow perched on a power pole cawed, the noise raucous and bleak. Marta thought for a moment of her rock dove and her mink, and felt comforted. The memory of the visitations was a talisman, an amulet she carried with her. But she also felt uneasy. What did the visitations mean? Her sure belief that God was telling her something had not wavered—but telling her what? Simply that God was involved in her life, that God was with her? If so, his presence didn't seem to be improving things much. That was probably a blasphemous thought. She walked past the spruce trees noting the rainwater dripping from the branches. Maybe she should go to church. Maybe that's where she would find the answers. She had not been for many months. After going to services twice every Sunday throughout her childhood and teenage years, her attendance dwindled to one service a week in her early twenties, to once or twice a month in her mid-twenties, to once in a while these days. It was hard to rise early yet another morning of the week while her husband slept on. With a pang, she remembered her father's gentle expression of concern when she had announced her engagement seven years before. "Your mother and I want to encourage you to be involved in a church—for your own support and to contribute to others." She had said of course she would keep going to church. Matt was a spiritual person, even if he didn't believe himself. "You don't have to worry, Dad." On her last visit to her parents on Victoria Day weekend, they had avoided asking her anything about church at all, keeping all discussions light.

Church. Maybe that's where God would reveal to her what the visitations signified. Or maybe she should be able to figure it out on her own. As she drew near the beer tent, avoiding puddles and mud slicks in the grass, she thought of Jenn's questions. Should she leave her job? It might not make a difference, she thought. Even with summer vacation in its third week, the soundtrack of leaving songs still played in her head. Maybe her subconscious was telling her to leave Matt. But she had made vows. And she loved Matt. Why leave someone you love? Because he doesn't love you back, she answered herself. Yes, he does. Well, not enough, came the back-of-her-head voice as she spotted Matt, body bent toward Nancy, as intimate as a parenthesis, eyes crinkled in delight at whatever she had just said.

CHAPTER EIGHT

AT WATER LEVEL, THE BELT Line Sewer smelled worse than the Storm Trunk Sewer or the High Park Drain, which they'd visited the week before.

She'd balked at the entry point Oliver led them to, in the open field of Memorial Park, near Eglinton and Spadina. The light was fading, but they were visible to surrounding traffic and houses. "Can we get in somewhere else?"

"Yeah, but we'll have to go through a low pipe for about ten minutes. Like, low enough we'll have to bend over. Are you claustrophobic?"

"No. You?"

"Nope." He led the way into a treed area underneath a bridge at the bottom of a ravine steep enough to toboggan down, had it been winter. Through the flimsy fence, Marta could make out a car dealership and a streetlamp. The ravine bottom was dry, although the steep dip suggested that in the past, or maybe seasonally, water flowed through it.

Though this was only her third trip, the air wafting from the manhole cover smelled as familiar now as chalk dust and lockers. The scent—earthy, slightly off—triggered images of the subscapes, the urban underworld she was coming to know. "What is it that you like about this?" Marta asked Oliver, who was tugging at the cover.

Oliver glanced up with a grin, his fourteen-year-old trouble-maker grin. "You know me—I like poking my nose in where it doesn't belong. What about you? Why are you doing this—I mean, more than once?"

"The same, I guess. I like the extra dimension it gives to the city. When I walk around now, I think about what's underneath me." She stopped. "Do you want help?"

"No." He took a small crowbar out of his knapsack. Marta's heartbeat sped and she scanned for onlookers.

She chattered to calm her nerves. "It reminds me of when we went camping when I was little, and we'd set up the tent in the dark—the next morning, I couldn't wait to get outside and orient myself, figure out where I'd been all night, what it all looked like. That's how I feel. Like now I know what I've been walking above for years."

"Wanna go into a subway tunnel next? There are some really cool abandoned side tunnels and rooms." He heaved the manhole cover aside and motioned her down ahead of him. Now the smell was stronger, almost rancid.

"Maybe. Or into a drainpipe in my neighbourhood?" She eased her foot onto the rung.

"Hey!" came a voice from across the ravine. "Hey!"

"Go quick," said Oliver, his voice urgent. Marta pointed her head down to shine the headlamp toward the bottom as she descended. She clamoured down eight steps until she reached a surface. Someone saw us, she thought. Someone is going to call the police. She'd read in the paper about two men who had been seen climbing into a drain eight months ago or so—the onlooker had called the police, who had gone into the drains after the men. Caught them and charged them with trespassing and mischief.

Maybe it would have been better if Marta had scooted out of the tunnel, grabbed Oliver's arm, and run across the park, run back to the car. Then their only crime would have been opening the manhole cover. But Oliver was struggling to pull the heavy manhole cover into place above his head, and then scuttling down, sending dirt—or maybe it was only dust—into her eyes and open mouth. The manhole cover had closed with a sharp clang, and Marta was certain the onlooker, and maybe other people too, had heard. The clang echoed back from below. She moved her face down. She was standing on a metal platform, a narrow ledge with a drop on each side of it. Another ladder waited, but she paused. "Do you think he'll call the police?"

"I don't even know if he saw us. He might not have been yelling at us."

"It sounded like he was yelling at us."

"Even if he was, I doubt he'll call anyone. Probably thought we had permission. I'm not going to worry about it."

He had less to lose than she had, Marta thought. Each September she signed a form to allow her school to do a police check on her. It had seemed like a joke in the past.

"Maybe we should come up through a different manhole, just in case he's waiting when we come out. Do you ever do that?"

Oliver joined her on the platform. "Yeah. Last January I climbed up a different ladder than where I went in, but the cover was frozen or bolted or something." He scratched his hair beneath the strap of the headlamp. "There's also the possibility that a manhole will open in the middle of a street." Marta realized she hadn't yet considered that danger, exiting the drain into an oncoming bus.

Oliver took his raincoat out of his pack, pulled it over his arms, and zipped it up. The air was already cooler than the warm summer air a few metres above, but thick with the odour—compost, old diapers.

"Stinky," said Marta.

"Yeah. It didn't smell this bad last time I was down here."

Turning sideways, he eased himself onto the ladder that ran between the platform and the wall. It was narrow, and he passed Marta his backpack, reaching up for it once he neared the bottom. She squeezed down after him, glad she was unencumbered.

They stood in a tiny, square room with a tunnel leading westward. Marta shone her lamp ahead of her through the opening. Her pulse was still beating against her ears from the scare on the way in, and her eyes were still adjusting to the darkness, to the way the headlamp revealed what was ahead of her but kept the periphery black. She saw that the tunnel was horseshoe-shaped, flat on the bottom. And short. Maybe five feet tall. She was only two inches taller than that, but Oliver had to be six feet.

"I guess we should have come down in the field," she said. "I shouldn't have dragged you to this entrance."

"This will be fine." He gave her his imp smile. "All for one and one for all."

Oliver's words gave Marta a sudden memory of Matt in the early days of their marriage. A camping trip with outhouses she found revolting—just holes cut in the wooden bench, spiders lurking in the shadowy corners. When she got up to pee one night, he rose with her. "No, stay in your sleeping bag," she said. The glow of the flashlight had illuminated the amusement on his face. "I'm going to save you from killer spiders," he said. He held her hand in the cool night air. The sky was clear, and the stars glowed. She remembered the sweetness, the pleasure of being indulged.

She shrugged, a physical movement to expel the memory. Matt was out with a band tonight—a married duo, so at least she could avoid her usual pang of anxiety about his doings. Not that she thought he was being unfaithful to her, not physically at any rate. Not yet. She gazed at the low ceiling of the tunnel ahead of them, feeling uneasy. Oliver would have to crouch the whole way. She watched him—he was changing the battery in his headlamp, struggling with the shrink-wrapped battery packaging.

She was reconsidering the whole enterprise. The darkness, the enclosed space, the rank-smelling water—none of these spooked her. But getting caught. The trouble she'd be in. The humiliation of it. Being called to account for her behaviour at work, trying to explain to Matt. "I'm wondering if this is a good idea after all," she said.

"What?"

"Being down here. Draining." Her voice sounded sheepish.

Oliver shone his flashlight in a full circle. "It's pretty isolated, isn't it? You definitely shouldn't travel down here alone." Oliver tucked the empty wrapping into his backpack and fitted the headlamp around his ears. He stepped forward, bending from the waist and neck. "If you fell, no one could hear you call. Who knows when you'd be found."

Marta stepped into the water behind him. The irony almost

brought a smile. It was being found, not lost, that worried her. She tipped her chin toward her neck and followed him. The murky water flowed past her heels and around her feet, cooling them through the rubber of her boots. She was relieved to find that, as in the High Park Drain, the surface was flat. The wading was still slow and slippery, but she felt far steadier than she had on the curved bottom of their first drain. Her stoop was so slight that occasionally she forgot to keep her head down and felt the roof scrape against the hood of her raincoat.

Like the Storm Trunk Sewer, this section of the Belt Line had long stretches of featureless concrete. The High Park Drain had a curved brick ceiling, which had seemed exotic and antique to Marta, although Oliver had told her it was built less than a century ago. The Belt Line Sewer, he had explained, was constructed in the late 1800s, built to drain Forest Hill. It ran beneath a ghost railway track, the former Belt Line Railway, an 1890s endeavour to link the suburbs to downtown Toronto along a circular route. The project failed early on, but the corridor still ran above the drain as a multi-use path through Forest Hill and westward.

The tunnel they were in was an add-on, a modern conduit beneath Eglinton Park, hence the smooth, pale walls. But there were interruptions to the grey surface. Tiny tunnels, the width of Marta's arm, dotted the walls. Several of them had rockflow beneath the mouths, the rock patterns fanning down the wall and intruding onto the flat concrete of the tunnel. The complex pattern of rock looked as preposterous to her as the sandstone hoodoos in the Alberta Badlands, not far from her childhood home.

They passed a ladder with another access point up above them. "Where does that lead?" Marta asked.

"I think we're right underneath that street south of the park. I don't know the name of it." As if to confirm his reply, a clang resounded from above as a vehicle drove over the cover. Marta cringed.

Occasionally the tunnel curved briefly; sometimes there was a much smaller, parallel pipe in the tunnel, alongside the floor, which Oliver said carried sewage. Water dripped into the tunnel from connections along the way, and, again, they passed flowstone that had created oddly beautiful formations along the edges of the tunnel, solid ripples of rust-coloured rock.

When she observed the water, though, any resemblance to pure or natural beauty disappeared. It flowed thick and muddy, and Marta soon suspected the substance eddying alongside her boots was not mud but waste. Oliver confirmed the thought. "The sanitary sewer overflow comes in here. Probably accounts for the smell too. It wasn't this gross the last time." Marta shone the light downward and made a note to clean her boots outside with the hose when she got home.

Soon after her neck began feeling uncomfortably stiff, the tunnel opened up into a small concrete room in which they could stand upright. Marta paused and did a few head rolls. Two tunnels continued from here, a small one too narrow to get into and a larger one. A previous explorer had graffitied enormous pink lips around its circumference so that it looked as if travellers who chose to continue were walking into a gigantic throat. The artist, Marta noted, had been adept with spray paint—the mouth was both sinister and funny. A wall at hip-level separated them from the entrance, and Marta followed Oliver in springing over it. Well, Oliver sprang, and Marta hoisted herself. She added fitness classes to church services on her mental list of things she needed to return to. They soon came to a little, square room with more artwork: a monkey face, graffiti tags. Marta scrutinized the artistry. "Not as good as that mouth," she called to Oliver's back.

"Maybe we should bring some spray paint next time we come down here. You can add vandalism to your list of crimes."

As she laughed, she realized that not only was her heart rate back to normal, but she was enjoying herself, revelling in the clandestine adventure. As long as she avoided thinking about re-emerging, she felt the high of exploration that belonged, she thought, to mountain climbers, deep-sea divers, cavers. Not usually to her.

From this room they took a step down through a low, square cut in the wall. And now they were in the large tank that Oliver had told her about. A huge chamber. Actually four side-by-side chambers, built as storage tanks for excess water. This was the underworld that kept basements dry and playgrounds from turning into ponds during intense rainfalls.

The room was enormous, longer than a subway station, about six metres across. High, though she didn't know how high. Oliver had estimated that they were about nine metres underground. She counted the steps of the access ladder and did her own calculations. That seemed right to her.

"Let's go to the next tank," Oliver said. He was already climbing up an access ladder toward the window-sized opening.

She followed him, feeling awkward as she ducked through and simultaneously turned her body to get her foot on the ladder of the second tank. This room was identical to the last, a huge, shadowy chamber. Oliver headed directly to the opposite side. "No ladder here," he called to her. She shone her light his way and saw windowlike openings chest-high in the wall. "I'm going over," said Oliver, hoisting himself up and onto the ledge with athletic grace. Marta knew that her arms were not strong enough to get up herself, and she didn't want to ask Oliver for help. It was okay to be alone here. The surface she was walking on was a few centimetres of mud, which she sank into slightly. It really seemed to be mud too, and the smell was back to root cellar, not sewer. The acoustics were incredible. Reverb that dazzled the ear. She hummed a tune that came to mind, then listened to the hum of her voice travel across the chamber and hit the far walls and ceiling. She sang the words.

> Should auld acquaintance be forgot
> And never brought to mind?
> Should auld acquaintance be forgot
> And auld lang syne!
>
> For auld lang syne, my dear,
> For auld lang syne.
> We'll take a cup o' kindness yet
> For auld lang syne.

"What does that even mean, 'auld lang syne'?" Oliver shouted from the chamber next to her. The words echoed throughout the chamber.

"Old long since," Marta called back. *Old long since*, the walls called back with a ping-pong delay, like a ball ricocheting, the notes and consonants increasingly muddied as the sound waves disintegrated.

"That doesn't make sense."

Sn't make sense, sense, sense, the walls affirmed. Marta listened until the sibilance mellowed and stopped.

"A less literal translation would be—'for old time's sake.'"

Oliver's head appeared at the opening between the two rooms. "Sad tune, kind of. You have a great voice."

"Thanks." Even at the lower volume, the consonants pinged and ponged through the cavern.

"There are two more rooms on the other side of this wall. You okay for a bit if I go have a look?"

"Of course. Take your time. I'm going to keep playing with the acoustics." She waved her fingers as his head dropped from view.

She turned off her headlamp. It was darker than night, especially Toronto nights, where light spilled from streetlamps, fluorescent signs, windows, and headlights. She stayed still—the black kept her pinned, although she had already examined the floor and knew it was only soft, grey mud, no doubt very fertile, with the decomposing waste mixed in the dirt. Her pleasure turned unexpectedly to sorrow, the way it had, she remembered, that day in the ballroom of the King Edward Hotel. The sadness stung her eyes, and she flicked her light back on. She moved around in a circle, taking in the expanses of grey wall, the grey floor, and, up high above, the grey ceiling. What was she going to do? Right now until Oliver returned and for the rest of her life? The urgency to find Aaron's letter had faded during the week as she did the readings for her course. On Wednesday evening she had gone out with her friend Lily, who observed that Marta seemed a little down. "Is it the course you're taking?"

"It's not helping." Her own sigh had surprised her with its length and depth. "Some of the people enrolled are so idealistic, and their comments make me feel like I'm cynical at worst, or underperforming at best."

Lily had leaned back, nodding her head. "There's this concept in my field called moral distress," Lily said. "I've only heard it applied to nursing, but it sounds like it could apply in your situation too. It's when you know what you should do but you don't do it because it seems impossible."

"Why 'impossible'?"

"You know—lack of time, too many other things screaming for your attention, lack of support. Oh, and institutional policies and the power structure, or even laws, that get in the way."

Marta thought of the fact that she couldn't check in with students over the summer, that she had to cut them off from the nurture she provided during the school year.

"So you end up feeling miserable because you dash through your work shift seeing what you *should* do, but not doing it."

"So what do you do if you have moral distress?"

"No idea. The term gets thrown around in the nursing station

from time to time, and we complain and wring our hands about it."
Lily fingered her crucifix. "I go home and pray. I use St. Francis's
words—you know, 'Make me a channel of your peace.'"

As Marta remembered the conversation now, she sang the words
of the song of St. Francis, very low, because she didn't want to have
to explain this choice to Oliver if he could hear.

> O Master, grant that I may never seek
> So much to be consoled, as to console,
> To be understood, as to understand,
> To be loved, as to love with all my soul.

The quick tempo of the song worked against her in the hall;
the reverb sent the consonants flying back in a sound as muddy as
the floor, all catapulting sibilance and bouncing sound. Ah, well, it
didn't ring true for her anyway.

NO ONE was waiting for them when first Oliver, then Marta
scrambled out of the manhole into the now-dark night. Nonetheless,
Marta said goodbye rather breathlessly to Oliver, and she scanned
the area furtively as she hurried toward her car.

Once she was south of Dupont, calm returned. She remembered
how she felt while she was alone in the overflow tank, the sorrow
and the indirection. With a decisiveness she recognized as unchar-
acteristic, she took a roundabout way home, driving past Bloor to
Dundas, then past Dovercourt to Gladstone. Here she turned right,
stopping in front of St. Anne's Church. The Byzantine structure

towered over the street. When she was researching the storm drains in her neighbourhood, she had read that it had been built in 1908 on what had been the bank of the Garrison Creek Ravine. The Garrison Creek, she knew, flowed imprisoned beneath her, buried alive since the late 1880s, when its pollution was deemed a threat to public health. She looked over at the building, noted the iron fence, the yellow brick, the white Byzantine towers with their copper roofs. She'd never been inside the church, but Chelsea, her art department friend, told her it contained religious murals painted by two Group of Seven artists. "They're impressive, if you like that sort of thing," Chelsea had said. It was neither the murals nor the unusual architecture that pulled her there tonight. It was the series she had noted on their signboard when she and Matt had walked home from a show at the Gladstone Hotel on Queen Street two weeks before. A summer series on Dame Julian of Norwich and suffering. Yes, there was the sign. *Transforming Grief: Julian of Norwich Speaks to Those Who Suffer. Tuesdays at 7:30 PM. Everyone welcome.* The series had started last week. Maybe they would let her come anyway. Churches were good that way.

Marta turned off the ignition and sat still. She pictured the water flowing underneath her through its red-brick prison, one of the oldest sewers in the city. She hoped to see it sometime. She looked at the sign again. Two pigeons fluttered nearby, but neither landed on the sign. No mink scampered by either. What do I do next? Marta wondered. She fiddled with her wedding band, absently shifting it back and forth. She noticed her fingers doing their choice dance in her palm, and silenced them by making a fist.

CHAPTER NINE

"MARTA! MARTA!" IT WAS MATT'S voice, and she turned toward him, opening her eyes with the effort of uncorking a bottle. "You're dreaming, hon. It's okay."

She was tangled up; she was trapped and had been calling out, panicked. "Did I wake you up?" Light glowed behind the curtains, but it felt early. She was soaked, felt the sweat on her face and neck, under her arms and breasts. Was still orienting herself. Toronto. The bedroom she shared with Matt, her husband. She twisted herself out of the damp sheet wound around her.

"You were tossing and mumbling. Couldn't make out what you were saying. A bad dream?"

"Yeah."

"What was it about?" He sounded more curious than concerned.

"Ropes. Knots." The details were already receding.

Then Matt surprised her. "Didn't you tell me once that that old boyfriend of yours—the crazy one—was into knots?"

"Yes. I don't think he was crazy, though."

"Of course he was. Only crazy people kill themselves."

Marta rose. "I'm going to take a shower. Sorry for waking you up."

"No problem. I have work to do today anyway."

Marta paused in the doorway. "What kind of work?"

"This and that. I'm talking to a guy about an investment deal." Eyes flitted toward the window, cats evading reach.

"Investment deal?"

"A warehouse that could be converted into rehearsal spaces."

"We don't have money for an investment deal. We're just making our rent and utilities bills."

Eyes on her now. Belligerent. "Well, this would be a way to get ahead. It's a money-maker. But I'd need you to be on board. You'd probably need to co-sign the loan."

"I don't want to co-sign a loan. I don't want to get involved in this." She surprised herself. Her fingers were in her palm, in position for the yes-no, yes-no dance, but they stayed still. The horror from the nightmare fuelled her anger.

"Don't you want us to make more money?"

"Yes, but I don't think a warehouse will make us more money."

"Don't you want to support me in my career?"

What career? she thought, surprised again at the condemnation she felt. She turned toward the bathroom.

"By the way, where were you last night? I called home and you didn't answer." Matt's voice seemed loud.

"Out with a former student." She moved to the dresser and rummaged for clean panties and bra.

"Who? What's her name?"

"His name." Her voice was flat. "Oliver."

"How did you and *Oliver*"—he stressed the name—"spend your evening?"

Marta sank onto the bed beside him. She heard Mr. Pereira's

Honda Accord drive away, and thought briefly about the Honda Civic she had driven years ago. Her first car. It was worn and damaged when she got it—needed new brakes, new tires, some bodywork on the front end. Then the transmission went. She nursed it for three years, though she knew she was a walking bull's-eye each time she had it towed to the smirking mechanic close to her apartment on Grace Street. She wondered now why she had felt so reluctant to dump the car, been so anxious to keep it on the road. She turned to Matt and observed him coolly. Reflections wafted forward from a level of consciousness she usually kept lidded. She considered the future she looked forward to—an intimate marriage, children, financial well-being. A mirage? That meant that the romantic past she believed in was probably idealized.

I must have PMS, she thought.

She took Matt's hand, and, worry on his face now, he let her. "I've been doing urban exploration." Her voice was factual.

"What's that?"

"Going places you're not allowed."

"Not allowed?"

"Places no one's allowed. Subway tunnels. Drainpipes. Abandoned buildings."

"What the hell?" He let go of her hand and hoisted himself up to sitting.

"Yeah. Well, so far I've only been in drainpipes."

"Drainpipes. Underneath the ground."

"Yeah. Underneath the ground."

"How do you get into them?"

"Manhole covers." She watched reactions flit across his face.

"Why?" More curious than angry.

"I'm not sure. Oliver invited me, and I really wanted to see what was there." Her voice faltered. She had prepared explanations, but they were for Jenn, not for Matt, and they didn't translate, wouldn't make sense to him, not with how little she and Matt communicated these days. She would have to start so far back to get him to understand, if that was even possible. "I saw . . ." She stopped, sighed instead of continuing. He'd think she was crazy if she told him about the signs. If she told him how often she thought about the mink and the dove and the secret places of the city while going about the mundane minutiae of her days. That she fingered the memories with the pleasure with which one recalls the details of a night of lovemaking.

"You and Oliver have something going on?"

Out of the quicksand onto firm ground.

"No, love. He's just a kid. Nothing going on." She felt grateful for his jealousy. That he still felt jealousy where she was concerned. Although she told herself not to read too much into it. Men who cheated, even men who left their wives, still raged when their wives, or ex-wives, found someone new. It was a primitive instinct, more about ownership than love.

SHE TURNED the tap on full, the temperature hot, and let the water pour over her skin. She willed the fragments of the nightmare to drain from her psyche. The knots. She thought about her first visit to Aaron's bedroom. They'd slipped in from the kitchen after his parents went to bed, and she had flinched as the door squeaked and clicked shut. Her eyes had sprinted to absorb the details of his private space—the navy bedspread, a poster of Alanis Morissette and another of U2. Odd pairing, she had thought. *The Sailor's Best Book of Knots* on his bedside table. Then he kissed her, lips fumbling at first, tongue surprising her. Her back stiffened but only for a moment. Her body, acting separately from her mind, drew nearer to his clutching hands, and the items around her faded to backdrop.

Later, in late winter or early spring, he bought rope—thin-gauge rope—and wound it into various knots. He told her the names. The reef knot, the bowline, the clove hitch, the sheepshank. And then nooses. Perfect miniature nooses. After they broke up, he attached one to the zipper pull on his pencil case where it dangled through May and June, macabre but appealing. No odder than a skull and crossbones on a binder.

Matt was gone when she stepped into the kitchen, and there was no note. Marta wandered to the desk in the living room and dialled Jenn's number.

"Hey. Want to come over?"

"I'm going to church this morning."

"Okay. Just wanted to talk to you about some things." Marta took a breath. She had intended to confess the underground exploration over a cup of coffee, or, better, during an intimate tête-à-tête some evening, with a bottle of wine. Maybe she should tell Jenn on the phone. Instead she said, "I'm thinking about taking a course on Julian of Norwich."

"Who's Julian of Norwich?"

"The mystic. Fourteenth century, I think. She had visions when she was thirty"—my age, thought Marta—"and then spent the rest of her life figuring out what they meant. Dad had that plaque on the wall of his study with her words, remember?"

"Yeah, I remember now. 'Behovely.' 'Sin is behovely but all shall be well and all manner of thing shall be well.' Something like that. I thought you were taking a course for work already. Why are you going to study Julian of Norwich?"

"Well, it's at a church. More like a discussion group. On suffering." Marta waited, feeling her palms dampen.

"Whose suffering?" Jenn's voice had that laser quality to it now. "Is it personal or general?"

"I don't know. I haven't gone yet. I'm just *thinking* of going."

"Well, it would be good if it were personal. I know you don't like to examine your feelings"—Jenn sounded cautious—"but . . ." She stopped, and Marta realized she didn't dare to continue, didn't want to offend Marta, or prevent her from going.

Finally, Jenn said, "I don't know whether Mom and Dad should have let you drop out of therapy all those years ago. Seems like it might have been a good thing."

"It wasn't." Marta paused, remembering. "Maybe we can go out for a drink tomorrow night. I have a few things I'd like to talk to you about. I'm thinking of visiting Lethbridge." Now where did that come from? Marta's mind floundered around trying to think of a way to retract those words.

"Wow. Okay. Tomorrow night. Let's meet at Drift. If it's too loud, we'll go somewhere else."

Marta's hand remained on the phone as if it were a connection to Jenn after she had hung up. Did Jenn think she was crazy? Jenn wouldn't use the word *crazy*. Though direct, she was also sensitive. Okay, then. Did Jenn think Marta was mentally unstable? Maybe she was. But since when? Since high school or more recently? She recalled the months after Aaron's death, her father's perplexed sighs, the music he played for her, her mother's worry. And then, Aunt Bea. Marta let go of the phone and sat back in the chair as she remembered that visit. About six months after Aaron's death, Aunt Bea, her father's sister, took advantage of a seat sale on Air Canada and flew in from Edmonton. Along with the pillbox that organized her medicines by time of day and day of the week, she brought painting supplies to capture the tropical flowers in the Allan Gardens greenhouse.

All of Aunt Bea's watercolour flowers, like the peony in the painting she gave Marta and Matt at their wedding, appeared faintly diseased or distressed, as though they'd received unpleasant news. Marta's dad always blamed Aunt Bea's hypochondria. Not only did Bea collect illnesses for herself the way other women acquired new shoes and purses—eyes glowing, urgency in her voice when she described the latest developments in her symptoms—but she also collected stories about other people's medical woes. She kept in touch with the relatives in Holland, cousins, second cousins, a few surviving elderly *tantes* and *ooms*, Marta's grandmother's younger siblings. She described them with reference to their physical limitations—Bertrand with the hump back, *arme jongen*—poor man; Maarten who lost his arm in a grain auger; Aagtje who had a breast removed. Aagtje was Marta's favourite to hear about. She had never met her and wasn't even sure how they were related, but when Aunt Bea said her name it sounded like a prolonged sigh. *Agh-yaaah*. But it was Aunt Bea who convinced Marta's parents to send her to a grief counsellor. "That girl is clearly *traumatized*. Do something! Maybe some anti-depressants or, who knows, she might even need shock therapy, you've left it so long."

So Marta had visited the Christian Hope Centre, in an office tower on the corner of Yonge and Eglinton. The woman that another hospital chaplain had recommended had been on maternity leave, and Marta got her replacement, a middle-aged woman with an angular face who made Marta think of Ole Golly from *Harriet the Spy*, so much so that, years later, Marta couldn't remember her real name.

Marta had found she enjoyed having someone who had to listen to her complaints and fretting, something her own mother had little time or patience for. She told Ole Golly how her family's car, a red Dodge, seemed to draw birds. No sooner had they washed it than it was once again bombarded with bird poop. Often her dad gave her a ride to school, and it was embarrassing to be seen in a excrement-coated vehicle. After a few sessions, Ole Golly, a touch of exasperation in her voice, had advised Marta to focus on the real problem. "Picture all your minor worries as strands of embroidery thread that you can easily slip to the side. Slip them out of the way and focus on the main reason you're here."

That was when Marta began picturing the real problem as a thick snake that curled from a branch where she'd woken it from its embroidery thread tower. It wanted to suffocate her in its coils and swing its hard, scaly tail at her the way dragons do. She refused to go back to therapy.

Marta rose from the desk and re-entered the kitchen. She made herself a cup of chai tea and poured Cheerios into a bowl, adding milk from the pitcher Matt had left on the counter. She wondered if he'd left it out on purpose, knowing that she detested room-temperature milk and was paranoid about it spoiling. Had they stooped to that level of animosity now?

She should have taken her cereal outside, eaten it in the sunlight and the birdsong, she knew, letting the summer breezes blow away the last wisps of the nightmare she'd had. But she sat in the empty kitchen and watched the minutes change on the microwave clock.

THAT NIGHT, maybe because she was meeting Jenn the next day, Jenn who would batter her with questions, she tracked down Mr. Maas. As she had suspected, it was easy. She didn't need to go through church channels; she just entered his name into the whitepages.ca search engine. Henry Maas in Lethbridge. So he had retired there.

Phoning him took more thought and courage than finding his number had. She stared at the mink screensaver for a while, then opened a word document and typed in his name and phone number to save it for later. Her fingers fidgeted. Or maybe now. She picked up the phone. If he answered, she thought, that would be a sign it was meant to be—she was meant to talk to him. If he didn't answer, she would hang up, leaving no message, and she would rethink the plan. No plan. Impulse.

He answered.

"Uh, Mr. Maas, it's Marta Elzinga. I was your student in—"

"Marta! How are you?!" His voice, warm and warbly—even when he was younger—brought back memories of his classroom. Her and Aaron's classroom.

"I'm fine. I'm living in Toronto and I'm a guidance counsellor."

"Yes, I knew that. And married to a musician, I heard."

"Well, not exactly. A band manager." She could hear the tightness, the lack of approval in her voice. "But I'm calling because I got my letter last month—the letters we wrote in your class."

"I assumed that was the reason for your call. I always hear from a few students after I mail those letters out. It's a fringe benefit of the assignment—students getting in touch years after they graduate. Any surprises in your letter?"

She couldn't tell him that she hadn't opened it. "Uh, no, not really. I'm actually calling to ask you about another letter." The pause stretched long as she swallowed. "Aaron Wouda's letter. I wondered if you still have it or if you gave it to his parents."

Silence poured from the speaker as her heart drummed. Then she heard Mr. Maas exhale, and she pictured him—thirteen years older than the last time she had seen him, and he had seemed pretty old then. She realized she hadn't asked him how he was, or anything else about his life. Maybe that was always the way it was with teachers and students—a one-way relationship.

"I still have it. I went to Reverend Bergsma—the minister who came after your dad. I asked him what to do with the letter. He told me to read it and then decide. Said not to give what might be a loaded bomb to Aaron's parents when they were already so vulnerable—it was the day after the death." Mr. Maas stopped, and she heard him exhale again, the sound strained and emotional. "But I couldn't bring myself to open it. I already felt guilty—like how could I have missed that he was so unhappy? I was afraid of what was inside. And I felt like that would be one more injustice to Aaron—to read his private letter when I promised all of you that I wouldn't read what you wrote. So I filed it with the rest of the letters and managed to forget about it, until I hauled out this year's stack of letters for mailing."

He stopped. Marta's temperature had shifted with his words, hot, then cold, now hot again. She felt odd, like she was having an unusual experience, unusual, at least, for her. The experience of being in the right place at the right time. *Serendipity*, she thought. That's the word.

"Mr. Maas, I would really like to read that letter." The sentence came out a bit breathless.

"You dated him, didn't you?"

"Yes. We broke up a couple of months before he—before I moved to Toronto."

"Did you have any idea he was so unhappy?" Marta flinched, then heard that his tone held no accusation or sting, just sorrow that had grown old. Mr. Maas, she saw, carried his guilt and sadness as she did. A fellow Sherpa, burdened with the weight, responsible for hauling the emotions to every experience since that death. If they were in the same room, she thought, maybe she would have touched his hand in a gesture of comfort, if she dared.

"I should have."

"You haven't been able to let it go?"

"Sometimes I think I have. Not lately, though."

"I don't know. About the letter, I mean. Whether that has any integrity at all, letting a classmate of his read it."

And this was like the book slamming shut on her finger just when the secret that drove the plot was going to be revealed. She breathed away from the phone for a moment. "What if you read it, and just told me if it tells us anything we didn't already know?"

"Can I think about it? I wonder if I should just give the letter to Aaron's parents. Tell them I mailed all the rest this year; that's why they're getting it now."

The guidance counsellor in Marta came to life. That was an awful idea. She pictured Aaron's parents fumbling with the envelope, tearing it open. Whatever conclusions they'd reached in thirteen years, whatever closure they'd achieved, could be undone. "Could be a real shock at this point. Like a message from the grave. It's different for you and me—we've known about the letter all along."

"You're probably right. But I don't know about reading it. In all the time I've been doing this, I've never opened a letter. I have six years of letters to be mailed out yet—I'm retired, of course, but I have them filed by year so that every student I taught will get theirs."

"Well, will you think about it? I seem to be at a place where I need more answers. Where I'm tired of going on with the questions." She felt the pull of the questions, the way they held her back. Maybe it wasn't only Matt, she thought. Or PMS.

"I'll think about it. Give me some time. Give me your number if you want, and I'll call you."

SHE MET Jenn at Drift, a newish bar on a strip of Bloor that seemed too derelict to include this inviting space—tables made from old bowling alley floor, the exposed brick and vintage signs, the plants. They sat at the table in the front window, looking across at Strickly Salsa.

"It's not bad enough that they've spelled it STRICKLY SALSA on their sign—Look in the window: their website is stricklysalsa.com."

"Maybe they meant to spell it that way," Marta said. Because of her immigrant students, she tended to be softer than most people about spelling and grammar on signs. How well could most Canadian-born Canadians spell in a foreign language? Most of them couldn't even write a sentence correctly in French, even after years of studying it.

"I doubt it," said Jenn. But she changed the subject. "Tell me more about the course you're going to take. The Julian of Norwich course."

"No more to tell. I missed the first meeting, so I don't even know if I can still join. It was just a thought. Something I thought might be interesting."

"All right. Then tell me about Lethbridge. Why on earth are you thinking of going there? Who would you even visit? You haven't kept in touch with anybody, have you?"

"Not really. Christmas cards with Lisa Van Akker and Allie Kort."

"Christmas cards don't mean they'd want you showing up on their doorsteps."

"No. I'd probably stay in a hotel." Actually she hadn't thought at all about what she'd do. Until her announcement to Jenn on the phone last night, she'd been unaware that she was planning a trip to Lethbridge.

"Why are you going there at all? Does this have something to do with Aaron?"

"I think I need to talk to his parents."

"I'm sure they'd love to see you." The sarcasm sliced. "Mom told me about the funeral."

"Yeah. Well, they were grieving." That was the guidance counsellor voice again. The teenage girl that cowered inside her recoiled at the memory. She and her parents had flown out in time for the visitation at the funeral home the evening before the memorial service. At first she thought she was imagining the stares, the antagonism in the murmurings around her. Then her mother placed a firm hand on her shoulder. Her voice was tense. "Let's pay our respects and go. Your dad can get a lift to the hotel with someone else." She clamped her thumb and finger over her lips like a clothespin as she steered Marta toward the receiving line.

Aaron's parents looked older, and fragile too, like vases of baby's breath that had turned beige and brittle overnight. Marta rubbed the dampness of her hand against her skirt, then offered her hand to Mrs. Wouda, who had just finished hugging a stout woman who looked like her. Her eyes changed expression so suddenly and completely that Marta thought of comic book drawings, caricatures, emotion transforming a face so much it was barely recognizable. "It's your fault," Marta heard. Whenever Marta replayed this scene, the voice boomed through the funeral home, loud as a gym teacher's whistle. But probably Aaron's mother spoke in a normal tone. It was the force of the words, the change in timbre from the previous hum of condolences, that silenced the room and drew all eyes to them.

"I didn't—" She was going to say "do anything," but she stifled the words. She knew her catechism. There were sins of omission, not just commission.

"You don't know what you're saying," Marta's mother said, unclamping her lips and gripping Marta's waist. Mr. Wouda grabbed Mrs. Wouda's arm. "Now, Anneke," he said. Marta could not tell whether his tone was meant to placate or to warn.

Marta's mother was turning Marta away. Not turning—yanking.

"You didn't even email him back! He told us that. You could have saved him, and you shut him out!"

"You okay?" Jenn reached across the small table to touch Marta's hand. The warmth of her fingers made Marta realize her extremities felt frostbitten.

"They must have blamed themselves too." Marta rubbed her fingers together and wiggled her toes. "I read a lot about suicide in my guidance courses. Parents usually feel a great deal of guilt."

"Those parents had no feelings. They were the coldest people I've ever met. That's how I remember them. Arrogant. Certain they were better than us, remember?"

She did. Aaron's family were newcomers to Canada, lured to southern Alberta by the promise of good farming. They, along with a small wave of similar Dutch immigrants in the 1980s and '90s, sold their plots of land in Holland for high profits and came to Canada with their good business sense, their confidence with technology and modern operations, their comfort with business organizations—local and international. They were well educated, well travelled, intelligent, quick to adjust to life in Canada. At first they intimidated the old immigrants and their offspring, the old immigrants who had come after the Second World War, impoverished, their educations interrupted by war. Those immigrants had arrived suffering despair about Europe and their homeland, broken by the Nazi occupation, the deprivation and cruelty that characterized the 1940s and '50s in Holland. If they had hope for the future in Canada, it was somewhat desperate, certainly intermittent. Those old-timers, their farm-kid offspring, and the very young children of the third generation were the main constituents of Marta's father's church and the Christian school Marta and Jenn had attended. They were straightforward people, content with high school education and maybe a year studying liberal arts at the denominational Christian college in Edmonton, or studying agriculture at Lakeland or Olds College. No one considered school as a good way to learn farming, but people said a year away from home was good for kids, gave them a chance to spread their wings.

So the old-timers were suspicious of the newcomers. They felt envy at first, and eventually some grudging admiration. If the newcomers showed faith, if they were fellow believers, that helped a lot. Aaron's family were churchgoers and sent Aaron to the Christian school. His dad was polite. Ambitious in his farming.

He acquainted himself with the owners of the area's most profitable farms, was standoffish with others. His mother seemed too good for the rest of them. Dressed more fashionably, wore jewellery even on weekdays. Socialized only with other newcomers. Seemed cold. They were growing sunflowers west of Coaldale. Marta remembered thinking how incongruous that seemed. They were unlikely people to grow sunflowers—their house contained nothing sunny at all.

"Yeah, they were pretty cold," Marta said.

"Do you remember what Dad said about people in rough times?"

"He said a lot of things. Which one?"

"How good people help each other. They even put off their own grieving to be strong for someone else. Weak people blame others. Aaron's parents weren't only cold; they were weak."

Marta took this in passively. She wondered idly where that contrast put her. She blamed herself for Aaron's death. She didn't help anyone else through it. She was, in fact, still mired in the mess. Was still hyper-vigilant, as were all victims of trauma to some extent. But not usually for so long. Once, when she had tried meditation, she caught a few glimpses of her consciousness as it flitted like a hummingbird, or like a mouse with a cat in pursuit.

"So why would you want to go talk to them? What good could it possibly do? It's not going to bring Aaron back. It's not going to make you feel better. In fact, I'm pretty sure it will make you feel worse."

Marta thought about how she felt. The low-grade depression, the flatlining of her emotional life. One could always feel worse—she knew that. Things were never as bad as they could get. Just watch the news. So, yes, the trip could make her feel worse. Yet she doubted it would. It seemed the way forward. She was groping blindly. The path through grief and guilt was not straightforward—she could see that. She thought of her underground travels.

"There's something else I should tell you about. Something I've been doing lately." She took a breath as Jenn turned her spotlight expression on Marta. She fiddled with her wedding band and avoided Jenn's eyes as she talked.

"What the hell?" Jenn sounded a lot like Matt as she took in the news.

"I know, it's an—unusual—hobby."

"Hobby? Try *crime*! Why do something so weird? And risky? Why don't you—quit your job? Or leave your husband?"

"I don't want to leave him. I love Matt."

"That's not the issue."

"But you just said . . ."

"You know what I meant. Just that, if you need to do something radical, there are better ways to be radical!"

Marta looked around, glad that the noise level in the bar seemed to be cancelling out Jenn's high pitch and volume. "I like it down there. It's peaceful and . . ." She was going to add "healing" but didn't know how to explain that to Jenn. Or, for that matter, to herself. What made it healing? Or *what*, exactly, was it healing? "It gives me—perspective."

"To get perspective, you go for a walk. On sidewalks, above

ground. Or drive to the Scarborough Bluffs and stare out at the lake. Take the ferry to the islands and look at the city from there."

"That's escape, not perspective." Marta fell silent again, feeling the impossibility of explaining. How life above ground was knotted, but below ground it was laid out in untangled lines.

Jenn leaned forward. "I think you're going a little nutso here, Marta. I think you should see someone again. Let me ask around and see if I can get a good recommendation for you."

Later, as she walked home past the scent of Mrs. Pereira's roses, she decided it could have gone worse.

CHAPTER TEN

ON TUESDAY EVENING, MARTA SPED through her course readings so that she could go to the meeting at St. Anne's. "I'm going to a study series tonight," she told Matt, who was looking at a band's website—the Dead Assassins, not a band she had heard of.

"Really? With that guy?"

"Oliver?" She smiled at the thought of Oliver in a church basement discussing a fourteenth-century mystic. "No." She looked at his expression. Behind the faint hostility there was stress. "Do you want to come along? Or walk me there?"

He glanced at the computer screen. "New band I'm meeting with. From Halifax. Celtic. Great Big Sea wannabes."

"With a name like that?"

"I know. Let me get my coat." He grabbed his rain jacket, and Marta found an umbrella, the one with music notes falling like raindrops that Matt had given her for her birthday five or six years ago. He locked the door and took the umbrella to hold over her head. "What's the meeting?"

"A series on suffering and healing."

"Something for work?"

"More for me. Personally." She felt his eyes on her. Her eyes watered, and she wiped at them furtively, a quick swipe, knowing he would notice and she wouldn't be able to explain. Mostly it was the fact that he was looking at her—no, it was how little he seemed to look at her lately, really look at her. It felt like the old days, to have his eyes turn to her with concern, like she was his to worry about. He shifted the umbrella to his right hand and took her hand with his left. They walked in silence. She kept her gaze down, avoiding puddles and the worms that had been flushed out by a full day of rain. Matt left her at the front doors of St. Anne's, his kiss more lingering than usual. Or maybe she had imagined that.

She entered the church, expecting that there would be stairs leading down—events like this were held in basements with stained carpets and the contradictory smells of commercial cleaning chemicals and mildew. But there was no staircase, at least not here. She moved forward, then gasped—in a hushed tone, suitable to the setting—as she saw the interior of the church. Colour pulsed from walls and windows and ceiling and floor—mellow tones of rose, beige, blue, and gold. Her eyes flitted to take in the profusion of paintings, stained glass, mosaics, and carvings. Every surface was decorated. The Byzantine dome drew her eyes upward—she estimated that it was twenty-five metres high. It was rich blue, adorned with murals and shimmering gold stars. COME VNTO ME ALL YE THAT LABOVR AND ARE HEAVY LADEN AND I WILL GIVE YOV REST, she read. The *V*-shaped *U*'s were jarring, but the letters glowed. Animal sculptures—peacocks, griffins, lions—added both whimsy and majesty to the scene.

She realized she had walked forward while gaping at the dome, and she now stood halfway along the aisle. She glanced toward the front of the church, where a few people had gathered in the chancel, perhaps the church leaders holding a meeting, she thought. They hadn't started yet—there were two women standing and chatting, and a few others sitting in the circle of chairs, one of them talking on her cellphone. Marta strolled toward them, planning to ask where her meeting was.

A lean woman with straight brown hair in a neat, short cut moved toward her as Marta ascended the stair to the chancel. The woman wore navy dress pants and a linen blouse in pale apricot. Glasses finished the tidy appearance. Jenn would have said she looked Anglican. It wasn't that she looked like Marta—her own clothes were a little more bohemian and loose, her hair less tidy, with those lettuce ends growing slowly into jagged tendrils—but Marta recognized the earnest expression, the grave manner. This woman looked the way Marta did in unposed snapshots. "I'm here for the Dame Julian series," she began at the same time that the woman said, "Are you here for the Julian of Norwich series?"

"Yes. Is it that way?" She looked to the side where she could see a hallway and an exit.

"No, you're in the right place. Sometimes we hold our events in St. Anne's House next door"—she gestured toward the hallway to the side—"but we've been trying to make this area"—she waved a hand casually upward—"a more public space, get more use out of the beauty. I'm Kathy Stewart." Now the hand came toward her.

"Marta." She shook Kathy's hand. "Marta Elzinga. I missed the first session. Is it okay if I sit in tonight? I won't talk—I'll just listen, since I wasn't here from the beginning."

The woman—Rev. Stewart, who, Marta had read on the church's website, was both an ordained priest and a professor—assured Marta that she was welcome. Welcome to join late and welcome to join the discussion. "This is very informal. I'm going to tailor the discussions to people's interests," she said, adjusting her glasses. Her smile softened her features. "Was there anything in particular that interested you in Julian, or something that you hoped we would talk about?"

Marta's eyes stung again. Get a grip on yourself, she thought. "Oh, no, I'm just here to listen in. My dad had a quotation of hers in his study."

"Let me guess—'All shall be well, and all shall be well, and all manner of thing shall be well.'"

"Yes." She considered adding that the plaque on her father's wall had included the opening to Dame Julian's sentence, the "sin is behovely" part before the "but all shall be well." She felt her own ignorance deflating her. Probably she knew Julian of Norwich the way her students "knew" Freud as the caricature of the psychologist with a patient on a couch, or the way people "knew" Shakespeare—could name the title of a few plays, knew the line "To be or not to be." The minister—Kathy—was going to tell her that the popular quotation didn't get to the heart of Dame Julian's beliefs, that it was a misinterpretation, that it was good that Marta was here so that she could deepen her understanding.

"My favourite words that she wrote," said Kathy.

They sat in straight-back chairs—twelve people in all, three men, nine women, most of them over forty. Marta choose a seat that had empty chairs on both sides of it. She gazed at the walls and windows, still amazed by the dancing colour and texture around her. The bottom half of the walls in the chancel was a mosaic of deep indigo accented with golden stars. Above them, stained-glass windows glowed—most of them featuring apostles, from what she could see. Two regal sets of organ pipes hung alongside the windows in the front curves of the chancel—decorative only, she was sure, since real organ pipes were kept in closets away from dust and fluctuating temperatures.

The woman on Marta's right took a bag of Peek Freans from a cloth tote and passed it around the circle. It went around twice, until a petite woman across the way from Marta stashed the box on the floor behind her. "Just holler if you want more," she said with a laugh. She was dressed in a purple Indian-print blouse that contrasted with the auburn ponytail swishing over her left shoulder. The easy smile and vivacious eyes made her appear to Marta like someone who had suffered little, and Marta wondered why she was here. Then she chided herself for this unfair thought—really, she knew better than that.

The two women on Marta's left were deep in conversation. The one farthest away was a heavyset brunette in her fifties, with a big bosom, big hair, and glasses large enough to be trifocals. The woman closer to Marta was a thin blonde—dyed hair, maybe? It looked darker at the roots, though Marta was no expert. She was younger than the woman she was talking to, but not as young as Marta. Her voice was soft and earnest. "I still have to live with it every day," Marta heard.

"It wasn't your fault," the brunette said.

"I was driving. Maybe if I had spotted him sooner. Or thrown on the emergency brake faster—if I'd had quicker reflexes. This is what I think about."

Marta bent down to fiddle with her sandal, which had gotten wet in the rain. She unfastened and refastened the strap, straining to hear.

"Have you gone back to work?"

"I can't even *ride* the subway, let alone *drive* it. I've been off work for four months now."

"Are you getting any help?"

"Yes. The Transit Commission has a program for—for us. Post-traumatic stress counselling. I'm still in it. This week my counsellor and I met at Yonge and Bloor and went into the station together. She said we would just stand on the platform together. It was terrifying. The sound of the train coming into the station. The brakes. I wanted to quit counselling right then. I don't know if I'll go back."

"I'd like to welcome everyone here," said Kathy. Her voice startled Marta. She straightened and fixed her eyes on the minister.

"Last week we talked about who Julian of Norwich was, and looked at whether we are to imitate her or merely to admire her from the great distance of the years that have passed and the differences between her experience and our own. We didn't reach any certain conclusions, so those of you who are here for the first time today"—she smiled at Marta—"should feel free to weigh in on that discussion yourselves. Before we start, since we've got two

new people here tonight, let's just go around and introduce ourselves. Your name and something else about you."

Marta's underarms grew damp immediately. She struggled
to come up with something as she listened to the introductions.
Something true but interesting. The auburn-ponytail-purple-
blouse was Fay, the other new attendee, and she was experimenting
with canning fruits and tomato sauces this summer. The bald man
next to her was Adrian; he was a bibliophile. Retired but busier
than ever with his book collection. The big-bosom-trifocals was
Shelagh with a "gh" on the end. She was working on an M. Div. at
U of T. "What's that?" asked the bald man. Adrian. "A masters of
divinity. I plan to become a priest." The thin blonde woman said
she was Juliette and was currently a stay-at-home mom.

"Your name is close to Julian," said Adrian. So what? thought
Marta.

"Mmm," said Juliette. She fiddled her fingers and looked down.

Marta's turn. "I'm Marta. Um. I'm a guidance counsellor."

"Where?" asked Shelagh.

"Dufferin Tech."

"Ooo—that's a rough school!" Shelagh sounded both repelled
and impressed.

"That's its reputation. Most of the kids are sweet." Marta realized she meant it. She didn't like strangers making assumptions
about her kids.

Kathy cleared her throat. "Okay. Julian was an anchoress, a
nun who lived in seclusion. She lived in a modest cell. She prayed,
examined her conscience, abstained from pleasures. She spent her

time, as the ancient words of St. Jerome put it, 'weeping for the world.' Last week, we talked about moral choices. Julian wrote about impure motives—that when we face a difficult choice our impure motives make neither decision defensible. Many of us took comfort in her words, 'It is enough to be sure of the deed. Our courteous Lord will deign to redeem the motive.'"

Marta felt distracted. She wanted to hear from Juliette. She contemplated talking to her afterward. Or waiting till next week, if she returned next week. She could ask her about the help she was getting. Who she was seeing. But she'd have to start the conversation first. She felt fresh sweat break out as she thought about approaching Juliette. Her eyes strayed up to the ceiling. She gazed at one of the paintings—the paintings Chelsea in the art department had told her about, created by Group of Seven artists. What struck her immediately was that the perspective was right: they had been painted with the viewer's position in mind, made to be looked at from far below. What struck her next made her head swivel rather suddenly and wildly as she scanned the other paintings and the dome above her. There were painted doves everywhere. Squatting on the eaves in the nativity scene. Fluttering above the donkey as Jesus rode into Jerusalem in the Palm Sunday painting. Hovering over the hole in the ceiling that the man needing Jesus's healing touch had been lowered through. Perched on the cross, one on each side of the crosspiece. And in the ceiling—doves were scattered throughout the swirling grapevines of the latticework.

"What we are in need of," Kathy was saying, "is not so much forgiveness but healing. In particular, we need to be healed of the idea that God is angry with us, and that we need somehow to obtain his forgiveness. He has already forgiven us. Dorothy Day summarizes Julian's message by saying, 'The worst has already happened and been repaired.' Your sin, my sin, your bad choice, my bad choice, is not the great tragedy or the primal fall. That happened with Adam, and it's already been fixed. Christ repaired it and restored it."

Adrian waved his hand and started speaking before Kathy acknowledged him. Marta did not follow his words; she had been staring at the dove on the right side of the cross, who had looked back at her serenely as Kathy's words reached Marta. Now she bent down to hide her eyes. Already forgiven. But in need of healing. She rummaged for a tissue in her purse. Funny, she thought, how when the body recognized a deep truth that the mind could not accept, the body reacted with tears.

At the end of the meeting, Shelagh rose and strode over to Kathy. She reached her at the same time as Adrian, who had also bounded from his seat after Kathy thanked everyone for coming. Marta heard Shelagh say, "I just have a quick question" to Adrian. Then she delivered what sounded like the opening of a speech on the ethics of care and civic responsibility. No question seemed forthcoming. Marta glanced next to her. Juliette seemed to be waiting for Shelagh. Marta's eyes sought the doves above her. She shuffled to the chair on her left, pinning her arms to her sides to hide the perspiration blotches. "Hi, I'm Marta."

"Yes." Juliette looked wary.

"Yes. Well, um, I overheard you talking to your friend before we started. About the, the——" She had been trained not to use the word *suicide*. "About the death in the subway. I, um, lost someone that way too."

"A jumper?" Juliette sounded incredulous.

"No, I mean, I had a friend commit suicide." There, she said the word. "A close friend. A boyfriend. Well, he was a boyfriend, but I had just broken up with him." She stopped and looked at Juliette as if she had just revealed the answer to an urgent question that Juliette had asked.

"Wow. Recently?"

"No. A long time ago. But I still think about it a lot." Understatement, she thought.

"So, you don't get over it?" Juliette looked crestfallen.

"No, that's not what I meant. I heard you mention therapy. I was thinking that maybe if I had therapy, or if I listen really well during these talks on Julian of Norwich . . . if I had done these things years ago, I wouldn't be here now."

"I don't know."

"How does your therapy work, if you don't mind my asking?"

"Well . . ." The word came out as a sigh. "I need to get home. But we could talk another time," said Juliette.

A brush-off, Marta thought. Not only had she botched the opportunity to connect with someone who had a similar experience, but now she would feel awkward at the next meeting—Juliette would ignore her, or be polite in that arm's reach way that people used to maintain distance. "Okay. Maybe I'll see you at next week's meeting." She tried for a bright smile, her guidance counsellor smile.

"Well, why don't you give me your email address? I'll send you a link to a website with information about the therapy I'm getting if you want."

"Yes—that would be great." The plummeting hopes bobbed upward again. Juliette hadn't produced a BlackBerry or an iPhone, so Marta wrote out her address on a piece of notepaper and handed it to her.

Before Marta left, she looked once more at the paintings. "They are inspiring, aren't they?" said Kathy coming alongside her. Marta examined the painting of the manger scene, the rich tapestry of the wise men's robes, the warm shades of terracotta, gold, and brown, the cow and the donkey peering over the half-wall, their expressions conveying curiosity and more intelligence than their real-life counterparts ever did. Most of all, her eyes lingered on the three doves, lined up on the eaves, a snug row of small, plump creatures at the same height as the star in the sky behind the window. The star that guided the wise men to the baby. The doves were not looking at the baby or the star—they were perched in the upper corner of the stable, not something the viewer's eye was drawn to. But present.

"Comforting," she said.

"HOW WAS it?" Matt asked when she came home.

"Good. Interesting." She stashed the umbrella in the tiny closet at the front door. The rain had stopped, and her walk home had been cool and pleasant. She sat next to him on the couch. He turned off the TV with the remote.

"You don't have to stop watching," she said.

"It's fine. Just City TV news, and not much happened today."

"Hmm." She tried to think of something to say. The mood was benign. He was present, she could feel that. But they had lost the habit of speaking. Among other things. Weeks had passed since they had made love, and the last event had been awkward. He came quickly, then tried to bring her to orgasm, but tension pulsed alongside pleasure as he stroked her, and eventually she moved away from him. She was unsure whether he felt relieved that he could go to sleep or disappointed at the abrupt and incomplete ending to their lovemaking.

"How's your summer course?"

"Uh, good. Almost done. I have to write the final paper."

"What are you writing about?"

"Um, culturally sensitive strategies for helping students to overcome barriers in their career choices."

"What kind of barriers?"

"You know—stereotypes, their family's or culture's expectations of them, their limited language skills—all the problems my students who are newcomers to Canada have."

"That sounds like an awfully ambitious topic for a summer class essay."

"Yeah, well, it's only one tiny aspect of my job, just one of the problems I'm expected to solve."

"What do you mean, 'expected to solve'? Who expects you to solve all the problems in the world? You do! No one else does."

"I'm hardly talking about the problems in the world. Only the problems with my own students. Just the ones in my part of the alphabet. That's hardly 'all the problems in the world.'"

"I'm pretty sure that in your part of the alphabet most of the problems of the world are represented. I've heard you talk about poverty, gangs, mental illness"—he ticked them off on his fingers—"learning disabilities, family issues, language problems, interpersonal problems. And I'm probably forgetting a few hundred others that have come up just in the last year alone. You're going to be crushed under the weight if you keep taking it all on."

"Well, what am I supposed to do? That's my job—to advocate for my students and help them solve their problems."

"Help. Not do it all."

"Who else is going to?"

"You've got to have some faith that things are going to work out. They're great kids—you say that all the time. Smart kids, most of them. They'll figure things out."

Faith. Her agnostic husband was telling her to have faith.

"Maybe you're right." She subsided into an exhausted slump.

"You're sort of in your own world lately."

Her back grew taut. *She* was in her own world? How could he . . .

"I mean, I know I haven't really been asking you what you've been up to, but I feel like we're losing touch." The words were gentle. "I'm always here if you want me."

She sat silent. She suspected he was manoeuvring; the words were duplicitous, tendrils of a web designed to keep her compliant and yielding.

He took her hand. His was unusually cold. "Do you still want me? In your life, I mean?"

She gaped at him, the words a jolt. He sounded sincere, even vulnerable. His brow was furrowed slightly, his eyes squinting in worry. Even though she questioned her commitment to him from time to time, she felt shocked that he could imagine her as someone who might not want him in her life, as someone brave enough to leave. How strange that he thought she had such power in her. But was he sincere? She didn't know. She didn't think she had ever seen that nakedness that was in his eyes. She wondered if they knew each other at all. People, she thought, were like cities—you got to know the main thoroughfares, but there was a world of mystery beneath that remained off-limits, tenebrous.

Or maybe he was manipulating her. She sighed. Distrust was a wearying stance. "Do you want me in *your* life? Because it doesn't seem that way."

"Of course I do!" His voice sounded aghast.

A few short months ago, she would have been a dandelion seed attached so lightly to the stem that one more word, one more breath from him would launch her in any direction he wanted.

"I'm really tired. Let's talk about this tomorrow."

CHAPTER ELEVEN

FRIDAY AFTERNOON'S HEAT WAS THE sort that wilted ambition, so, rather than tackling the research for the essay due Monday, Marta switched on the fan and sank onto the piano bench. She played a verse of her lawnmower song:

> Your needs were cords that I bound to mine
> In a knot only God could untie,
> When you took my hand, our hearts entwined
> So tight that they chafe and they sigh.

It wasn't working; she knew it wasn't working. The whole song had to go, but she resisted throwing it out. Maybe if she tweaked the last line.

> Your needs were cords that I bound to mine
> In a knot only God could untie,
> Your hands were a noose around my heart—
> If I struggled I'd surely die.

That was better, although she didn't know what it meant, or who it was about. But it was better. Of course the lawnmower verse had to go. The whole song was liable to get very bloody if she didn't control the metaphors. Really, she wasn't much of a writer. Or a singer. Or a pianist. And it was too hot to be song-writing anyway. She turned on the bench to face the fan and pulled her blouse up to bare her midriff. The breeze felt moist and sullen, like the effort to make its way across the small living room was too much to ask. The landlord was against central air, had said Toronto's climate didn't warrant the cost. Made a remark about the environment, watching their faces slyly to see if that would prick their consciences. It worked for Marta, but Matt just stayed away on the really hot days, avoided the house and the overheated garage. Where he spent his time, she wasn't sure. Coffee shops, a friend's basement recording studio, the workout room at the community centre.

Marta moved to the computer desk and pulled up her email. She had spent the week waiting and hoping for news—from Mr. Maas, who still had not phoned back; from Oliver, who had talked about another expedition; from Juliette. And in spite of the way the heat was intensifying the force of gravity in the room, holding everything, including her, fast in its place, she felt restless. She pictured herself as a frog submerged in a cooking pot, the temperature heating up slowly enough that she would eventually die if she didn't act. Only she couldn't decide on an action. Or at least not yet. Decisions took time—or you could make mistakes. She remembered when Matt had surprised her with a proposal. She thought he had surprised himself too. There was no ring, just a spontaneous-sounding "Let's get married" one April morning over lattes in the Nova Era bakery on Bloor Street. "Wow. I need some time," she had said. He looked defenceless, one hand on hers, the other surrounding his mug. She spent the afternoon debating, wavering. Marriage seemed hasty; she felt uneasy about their relationship. It wasn't that he lied to her, but, occasionally, she sensed something shifty in him, like the way he had led her to believe he was a musician. Or maybe she had jumped to that conclusion, and was imagining the equivocation. But if she broke up with him—that thought made her even more uneasy. The hurt she would cause, the harm. She phoned him in the evening to say yes. Funny, the trivial decisions—which lip gloss to put on, whether or not to try bubble tea, which seats to choose at the theatre—propelled her fingers to twitch and squirm in her damp palm while in her head she recited, *Eeny, meeny, miney, mo*. But she'd made that decision in an afternoon.

Her inbox was empty. She opened her Google homepage and typed in *post-traumatic stress Toronto*. She clicked on one of the links, a PDF from one of Toronto's mental health organizations. It was a story, graphic-novel-style, about a boy from a war-torn country suffering terror when the fire bell rang in his Toronto school. Clearly, the illustrators weren't up on the latest in school law or the College of Teachers guidelines—the school employees, a teacher and a janitor, had their arms around the student, were shown touching his shoulders, his face. Or maybe the illustrators were taking a political stance, advocating that giving a human response to a panicking kid was worth getting fired for. Marta read on. The boy's classmates were a lot kinder than the kids she knew; their dialogue with the sheepish youngster after he knew he was safe struck Marta as about as realistic as a 1950s sitcom.

But the information below was helpful: *Do you have any of the following symptoms? Sleep problems or trouble with concentration, hyper-vigilance—that is, are you easily startled or always watchful? Intrusive memories, flashbacks, or bad dreams? Panic attacks? Feelings of guilt? Do you avoid places or things that remind you of the event? Do you feel emotionally numb and/or distant from other people? Do you feel frequently sad or hopeless?*

Below the list, the reader was informed that: *If you answered 'yes' to three or more of these questions, you may have post-traumatic stress syndrome.* Then it gave contact information. *Help is waiting for you.* In smaller font, the page warned: *If you put off getting help, the traumatic memories and the effort it takes you to guard against them will harm your functioning and decrease your pleasure in living.*

I could have written that, thought Marta. But so what? Everybody knew that knowing something didn't mean you were able to act on it. An obese person knew the fat slab of chocolate cake she was forking into her mouth wasn't good for her. But she gobbled it anyway. Idly, Marta wondered about the instant gratification in her case. What was the chocolate cake she got out of her safety mechanisms and coping techniques? She considered her indecision, the finger dance. She supposed it let her off the hook. Left decisions up to chance, or up to God—if he was interested in the trivia of her daily life.

The front door swung open. "Fucking hot in here," Matt said. He took off his sunglasses and dumped them on the coffee table. Marta quickly closed the computer window and, casually, reopened her email.

"What'cha doing?"

"Just checking mail."

"Anything interesting?"

"Nothing at all. I was hoping to hear from a woman I met at that church thing on Tuesday."

"Oh—yeah. You could use a few more friends."

If she had quills, they would have bristled. "What do you mean?"

"You only see your sister and sometimes Lily. Don't most women have more friends than that? I mean, it's up to you—if you're content, you're content." He put his hands up in surrender.

"Maybe if you were around more, I wouldn't need more friends."

"You don't want to do the things I want to do. You don't like going to clubs, you don't listen to music anymore, you don't like my friends."

"You mean your girlfriends?"

"What do you mean?"

"You know what I mean." Her pulse drummed in her ears. Their eyes locked like those of animals preparing for combat.

Matt's cellphone rang—the chorus from one of The Wheat Girls's songs. Marta left the room.

ON SATURDAY evening, around 9:30, Oliver rang the doorbell. "Oliver," Marta said in as hearty a voice as she could muster, "meet my husband. Matt, Oliver."

Though not as tall, Matt was broader than Oliver. He walked to the door, and using his width and his years, he loomed forward. "So you're the guy."

"At your service." Oliver bowed low from the waist, one hand over his heart, the other hand rolling in an extravagant flourish. The gesture, theatrical and grand, changed Matt's aggressive expression to irritation—the kind of irritation you feel about a housefly circling your head, Marta thought. She relaxed. Oliver had the skills of a darting insect when it came to sidestepping attack.

"You've got my wife breaking the law."

Oliver did a mock salute. "I'm just the tour guide, sir. Hey, Ms. E." He turned sideways to face her. "My friend George is meeting us. We should go."

"Where are you going tonight?" Matt's voice was gruff.

"Not far from here." Marta heard the excitement in her voice, a child unwrapping a gift. "Underneath Bloor Street and Dufferin Grove."

"Underneath the park?" Matt sounded interested in spite of himself.

"Yeah," said Oliver, "but we won't enter the drain there—that manhole is by the tennis courts. Too busy."

The entry point he chose instead struck Marta as quite well lit and peopled. She wondered if the tennis courts could be worse. They had walked west a couple of blocks on Bloor Street and turned north on Bartlett Avenue, a street that contained the usual west-end Toronto hodgepodge of century duplexes, some still in the original brick, shabby but sturdy. Others had fresh siding and wrought-iron fences painted white, or pre-fabricated brick, or false fronts made of stucco. At the corner of Shanley and Bartlett, George was waiting, and Oliver introduced them. George had the sinewy build of the kind of men who stay skinny their whole lives. He looked nervous, and Marta wondered whether the unease was caused by her presence or the evening's plans. "Have you gone into the drains before?" she asked.

"No. I'm more into subway tunnels. Oliver says once I've tried drains, I'll be hooked, though."

Marta observed the manhole. Its checkered iron cover rested in the sidewalk, exposed to the two streets, exposed to the porches, yards, and windows of the narrow Victorian houses on all sides. Though she lived on the other side of Bloor, this was her neighbourhood, and it was not the suburbs or even uptown, where residents went out for the evening or disappeared inside when the sun set. People in this neighbourhood lived outside in summer, especially during the long evenings. They fussed with their flowers, used hoses to nudge fallen leaves and dirt off their cement pathways, lazed on the front porches, laughing, arguing, drinking homemade wine. She noted the front yard just east of them, full of half barrels with pepper plants and tomato plants supported by sticks and twine. At any moment the front door could open; the gardener could step out to examine the hard green vegetables. A climbing rose fanned out along the fence across the street, deep fuchsia flowers blooming loud as trumpets. In this neighbourhood, dog-walkers meandered along sidewalks at 11:00 PM; people adjusted sprinklers and kids started street hockey games well into the evening.

They stood in the twilight, listening to the cicadas and crickets, a sprinkler, laughter from a yard nearby, someone on rollerblades swishing rhythmically along. Marta's tension rose. *Please don't let me get caught*, she prayed, wondering whether or not God would honour such a prayer, given that what she was doing was illegal. Illegal and not even necessary, like someone who stole a loaf of bread to keep his dying child alive. Not something she should bother God with, but she couldn't help herself. *I won't do this again if only you make sure I don't get caught this time*, she promised.

A man and his dog passed by, a small, compact man with a squat, wide dog. They waited. Two cars slid by, one driver glancing curiously at the three of them lingering on the corner. Then Oliver slid the lid open, and she shimmied down as quickly as she could, keeping her light off, hoping her feet would find the next step. Her foot dangled in the air—the ladder continued over to her right. She slid her foot, her hand, and then her body to the parallel ladder just below the one she was on. George was in the tunnel now, then Oliver, struggling with the lid. He made his way down. "Anyone see you?" she couldn't help asking.

"Someone drove by—stopped for the Stop sign. Doubt they'll care enough to report us, though." He shrugged. Marta felt perspiration dampen her forehead, though it was cooler here than it had been on the street.

But when she got to the bottom of the ladder and saw the tunnel stretching before them and behind them, she no longer cared. It was freeing to walk—so simple to just follow the tunnel. Especially when it widened and she could walk without stooping at all. She wanted to walk all the way to the lake. What a way to get to the lake. No traffic, no other pedestrians, no stoplights, no obstacles.

She took the lead and shone her new, bright flashlight forward. The tunnel looked like a worm with regularly spaced ridges circling it. It was smooth concrete, only around forty years old. The water was storm water, not sewage, the smell mild.

At Bloor the tunnel went sideways and down, and so did they, navigating a series of ladders, about three dozen big steps until they were far underneath the ground. In the awkwardness of leaving her house with Oliver, Marta had grabbed her raincoat without a hood, the one she wore to work when she carried an umbrella. After the first ladder and the rain of dirt and spray from the guys' boots above her, she gave up the lead. She slowed a little, torn between staying close to the only other humans in the underworld and her desire to be alone. South of Bloor the tunnel widened, and continued to widen, she had read, as it got nearer the lake and as more tunnels joined it. She found the monotonous view lulling. Occasionally there was refuse in the water on the cement floor. Marta noticed what looked like a licence plate. She nudged at it with the toe of her boot, but it was too covered in gunk to identify its province or year. Here and there stalactites hung from the ceiling, icicles of rock. Looking at them calmed Marta; they spoke of patience, of dawdling accretions and gains. Some things were accomplished at a rate too slow for the human eye to see.

Whatever was coating the shallow bottom of the curved tunnel, a silty substance, it held on to their footprints as they walked. Marta glanced back several times at the gloomy trail, imagined the prints as fossilized evidence of their visit. As always when she was underground, her sorrow was a tangible force, stinging just behind her eyes. But the pressure felt bearable. The sounds were so muffled. The occasional drone of Oliver's and George's voices, too far ahead for her to follow the conversation. Sometimes she thought she could hear traffic above them, but it was hard to know what the rumbles were. The only certain sound was running water.

"Where are we?" she asked. Oliver and George had turned and were sloshing toward her.

"Between College Street and Dundas, maybe? We haven't been walking long enough to be much farther." Oliver reached into a pocket and produced his cellphone. "Almost ten-thirty." He shoved the phone back into his raincoat. "We should go back. George and I have something else going on tonight." They had all switched off their headlamps to avoid blinding one another while they talked, and Oliver had his handheld light aimed at the water. Despite the shadowy dimness in the tunnel, Marta saw his eyes glimmer as he spoke. She studied George, who shifted his body weight and avoided her gaze. Best not to ask what the "something else" was.

"You guys lead," Marta said.

The trek back was noticeably uphill even before they reached the series of ladders deep underneath Bloor Street. Marta let her thoughts meander, and they meandered their way to Matt. In the safety of the muted tunnel, she reflected about love. It was like the air inside a house—it wanted to escape, to slip outside, she thought. When you opened the door on a hot day, the cool air rushed out. And on a cold day, especially in their house, the heat seeped out the cheap windows, the uninsulated roof, the cracks along the base-boards. It took both of you to keep it inside. Constant vigilance.

Or nurturing, if you wanted a nicer word. But they amounted to the same thing. She and Matt had been careless. Matt physically absent and intimate with others. She entangled with her past. She thought of her song. *In a knot only God could untie.*

The guys were well ahead of her when she reached the ladders. She thought she could hear Oliver, could just make out his laugh above the rumble of the water. She gripped the slippery rail. She'd meant to take along her gardening gloves, the ones with the leather on the palms. If she fell, Oliver would come back for her; she was certain of that. But it would be physically awkward, and even more emotionally awkward, to be lifted out and carried home by a former student and a young man she'd just met. She kept her pace slow as she climbed. Despite feeling cautious, she enjoyed having her companions far enough ahead of her that she didn't have to dodge grimy water dripping from their boots. Besides, she was savouring the time alone.

When she arrived at the platform at the top of the third ladder, she saw Oliver and George waiting for her, and she quickened her steps. She changed her mind about the speed almost immediately. Swift movement not only sent dirty water splashing upward, but it made her footing on the slippery surface precarious.

"It's over there," Oliver said when she reached them. He nodded his head forward, a motion that made the beam of light from his headlamp bop through the tunnel. He walked forward about thirty more steps, then stopped. They were back under the manhole they'd entered, a block north of Bloor Street. If it weren't dangerous to stay down alone, if she could get the manhole open by herself, she thought she'd like to stay awhile longer.

"I'll go first," said Oliver. He grabbed a rail and clambered upward.

"You can go next," said George. So Marta started up, keeping her head down to avoid the greyish water trickling from Oliver's boots. She heard him wrench open the manhole cover. She felt as if she were awaking from a nap; she resisted the urge to shake herself literally in order to escape the deep reverie she had been in during the walk southward and back. She was looking forward to the solitary walk home. With any luck, Matt would be out, or asleep already, so that she could slide into bed and drift off without more conflict.

"Shit!" she heard Oliver say, then saw arms grab him away from the opening. Her stomach twisted and her pulse sped, the body understanding the situation before her preoccupied mind grasped it. She climbed the last two steps of the ladder and heaved herself out of the manhole. The blazing lights of two police cars grabbed her eye first. Then she caught sight of the onlookers—the whiff of drama drawing neighbourhood porch-sitters and dog-walkers. Then, right in front of her, two police officers. The male officer was fifty-something, with a trim, fit body that defied the middle-aged cop stereotype and patient eyes that made her think about vice-principals that had been in the business for a very long time. The policewoman was her age, with short, dark hair in a pixie cut that did nothing to soften the grim expression on her face. Their weapons were not drawn, and neither of them touched her. Yet she felt terror.

"Miss," the policewoman said, "you're under arrest for mischief." It was like on TV. George had emerged from the manhole now, and both he and Oliver had been surrounded by other officers; they had been pushed against the cruisers. An officer was patting Oliver down. The policewoman motioned her toward the cruiser and gestured to it, as if she were ushering Marta into an armchair. Marta could see George's head pressed up against the top of the opposite side of the cruiser. The policewoman handcuffed Marta, then searched Marta's pockets and removed her flashlight and wallet. She was reciting Marta's rights. Marta could hear the words echo as Oliver and George, too, were arrested, then read their rights. She tried to pay attention—". . . to retain and instruct counsel without delay. We will provide you with a toll-free telephone lawyer referral service if you do not have your own lawyer. Anything you say can be used in court as evidence. Do you understand?"

"Yes," she managed.

"Would you like to speak to a lawyer?"

"Uh . . ." Her mind was sluggish, dragging like a kite caught in a crosswind. She wanted to shake her head to dislodge her thoughts, but she didn't dare to move. "I don't think that's necessary," she said finally. Oliver. He was just a kid. She needed to protect him. "We were down here because of me," she announced. "I asked them to take me."

"Put them in the cars," barked the male officer. Marta watched as George and Oliver, also handcuffed, were pushed into the backseats of the two cruisers. A young officer grabbed Oliver's backpack and groped through it. He held up the small crowbar Oliver used to open stubborn manhole covers. The older male cop near her raised his eyebrows. Craning her neck, Marta glanced at his uniform. Antonio Melo. *M*. She wondered if he was from the neighbourhood. He looked the right age to have teenage kids. She might be his kids' guidance counsellor. "I'll run the ID," the policewoman told him. She had pulled Marta's licence from her wallet.

"You can turn around," said Officer Melo. She wondered what rank he was. She didn't really know how police officer rankings worked. He was in uniform. She was pretty sure that un-uniformed cops outranked uniformed cops. The gun at his side drew her eyes. She looked into his eyes, still patient, even a bit tired. "What the hell were you doing down there?" he asked. She heard the slight stress on the *you*.

She was glad they left her her raincoat. It was probably above twenty degrees, but she felt shivery, as if she'd just had a car accident. "I'm feeling sick. Like I might faint."

"Sit down," he said. He moved his hand to rest on his gun as she sank down and sat on the sidewalk. It was awkward to sit with her arms handcuffed. She felt surprise that anyone could think of her as a threat. She faced the officer again and noticed another officer advising the onlookers to go home. "So, you were telling me what you were doing down there."

"Just exploring. It was my idea. I didn't dare go down by myself. They just came because I asked them to."

"Why did you want to explore the filth down there?"

"I don't know. I just wanted to know what was there. What was underneath the streets."

"Were you planning to try to break in somewhere? Dufferin Mall maybe?"

"No! Nothing like that."

"What about the boys with you? Up to some mischief? Planning to set off an explosion underground? Disrupt the subway maybe?"

"No—I told you. They were down there with me because I wanted to explore."

"Do you know you're not allowed to go down there?"

"Well, yes, but I didn't think anyone would mind. I didn't think we were hurting anything."

The barrage of questions continued, getting more repetitive as time passed. The policewoman came back. "Marta Elzinga, thirty, lives on Dovercourt Road. A teacher." The last said with disgust.

"Where do you teach?" asked Officer Melo.

"Dufferin Tech. I'm a guidance counsellor."

The officer laughed. "Look who we have guiding our young. No wonder they go astray."

Marta considered the humiliation she was facing. Her principal, her colleagues, her students. Matt. Jenn. Her parents. She wanted to scurry back into the manhole and stay there. Die a slow and private death of dehydration. She wanted Jenn suddenly. Maybe they would let her call Jenn. From the police station. She was allowed one call. Or maybe that was true only on American TV shows. She wondered if they would actually put her in jail, fill up crowded city jail cells with guidance counsellors caught trespassing.

"What did you say I was charged with?" she asked.

"Mischief."

"Is that a criminal offence?" Her voice wobbled.

"Yes, ma'am."

"Oh." She glanced at the four officers, who seemed now to be lingering, chatting. Maybe they could get on with things. How much time did it take to check records and take action? "Speed it up," she wanted to say. They should work in a high school for a few weeks. They'd learn how to get through the paperwork, keep things moving. "Chop, chop," she could hear her principal bellow as she plowed through the halls marshalling kids into their classes like she was clearing snow.

The police officers were having a hushed conference now, a ways in front of the car. She swivelled her head to look at Oliver, but she couldn't see him from where she was seated. She didn't dare rise. She had to pee, really had to pee. She wondered what the bathroom situation was in jail. The new Don Jail, which was far from new—that's where she'd end up after sentencing. Too bad it wouldn't be the old Don Jail next door. She'd love to see it, even if she were a prisoner. She'd seen it only from the outside. Built before Confederation, the jail had the formal grandeur of the public buildings from its time. An imposing stone carving of Father Time greeted both guards and prisoners on their way in. She'd seen photos of the impressive rotunda, from which the cell wings led off. There were balconies, catwalks, wrought-iron dragons and serpents. The cells were gloomy—like a medieval dungeon, she'd heard. She knew nothing about the new Don.

Would she have to pee in front of people? She often had trouble peeing if someone was in the stall next to her. Sometimes she flushed the toilet before sitting down so that the sound would muffle the stream of urine. Maybe if her bladder were about to burst, she'd overcome her modesty.

The police were still talking. One of them was writing on a pad. Marta wanted Jenn again, a thought that made her think of Matt. It was going to be excruciating to see Matt after this. He'd be full of glee, she supposed. "I told you so. What the hell were you thinking? And what is wrong with you these days? Why do you have to go *looking* for trouble?"

Officer Melo approached her. The other officers were opening the doors of the cars. The guys were walked over toward Marta, who stood up. Their cuffs were removed. George looked at her uneasily, like a cornered cat, but Oliver's eyes, Marta noted, were still glinting. She avoided catching his eye—he'd grin or do something that would put them in even more trouble. Now Officer Melo was talking. "We could charge you with mischief—you had no business going down in the tunnels. But we're going to give you a lesser charge under the Trespass of Property Act, which carries with it a fine." He handed out tickets to each of them. Marta scrutinized hers. Trespassing.

"Is this a criminal charge?" Her voice quavered like a child's on the verge of tears.

"No."

Not a criminal charge. And the fine was only sixty-five dollars. She felt like she'd received a ticket to a show, a winning lottery ticket. The relief made her knees feel weak again. She took several deep breaths through her nose.

"You're free to go. I don't ever want to see any one of you again, you understand?"

"Yes, sir," both Oliver and George said. They turned to walk away—south, toward Bloor Street.

"Ms. Elzinga." The officer's voice was stern.

"Yes." Wary. The guys paused. "Go ahead," Marta said to them. Just in case the officer changed his mind, she wanted them to get away.

"Especially you. You should know better."

"Yes, sir." She didn't have to feign the shame in her voice.

PART THREE

THE WAY BACK

And the way up is the way down, the way forward
is the way back.

—T.S. Eliot, "The Dry Salvages"

CHAPTER TWELVE

THE BEAUTY OF THE CHURCH pulsed over her, the element of surprise gone, but the joy of having her anticipation realized perhaps even more pleasing. Marta's eyes sought and found the doves as if she were finding old friends in a crowd. She paused in front of the chancel to appreciate the glowing windows, the way the light glimmered through the dark, rich tones of the coloured glass. Then she sat down in a chair with empty seats on either side, balancing out the semicircle. She nodded at Shelagh and Fay. Kathy was talking to a newcomer, and Juliette wasn't there. Looked like they were going to be a smaller group tonight.

Marta took slow breaths, striving for a serenity that, well, was always lacking, but seemed more remote than ever since her near-arrest three days ago. She looked around, counselling herself to relax. After all, this was a safe and appropriate place for a guidance counsellor, not to mention for a woman raised by good Christian parents. Not that she could muster any self-righteousness. Shame was still the dominant emotion, with bits of sheepish gratitude piercing through the mortification. Her name, her photo weren't in the newspapers. None of her students had sauntered by and joined the bystanders during the half-hour she spent in handcuffs on the sidewalk. The charge was not criminal; the fine was affordable, although not, obviously, in their budget. Matt had pointed that out.

She had stolen into the house at midnight, hoping he had fallen asleep, a deep sleep. She would creep into bed, stay far over on her side. Maybe tell him in the morning. But he was at the computer, watching YouTube videos. He merely raised his eyebrows when she entered. Weary, fragile, and ashamed, she realized he was perhaps the last person she wanted to see. Some people had spouses who supported them, to whom they hastened home after a bad day because, over a bottle of beer or a glass of wine, they could divulge the snags, the hassles, the strife they'd endured that day, and, in so doing, lighten the weight. She remembered her dad's rants when something upset his sense of fairness or his sense of decency, and remembered her mother's practical questions in response. At the time, she felt that her mother wasn't taking him seriously enough. She wanted her mother to get her back up, maybe rant a little herself in solidarity. She saw now how her mother brought balance to her husband's passionate stands—her questions soothed him, brought him down to earth, reminded him that this was a damaged world. Without judgment, she encouraged him to temper his response to the things that contradicted his values. Well, support wasn't Matt's strength. He was going to add to the humiliation, Marta knew it.

Somehow this miserable certainty had provided the strength she needed to communicate a factual summary. The subtext of her tone and body language said, "Don't mess with me tonight."

"Marta, what the hell is wrong with you?" He had shut down the computer and stood up. "I'm going to bed."

Kathy was now motioning the newcomer, a young, very fit woman, to a seat. Adrian arrived with a travel mug and his own copy of *Revelations of Divine Love*. Probably signed by Dame Julian herself, given how proud Adrian had sounded during the last session about his book collection. Adrian the bibliophile. Marta reproached herself—he wasn't very likable, but maybe there were good reasons for the way he needed to show off.

Then Juliette was walking up the aisle. She glanced at Marta, and Marta produced a smile. It was an ambitious smile—she tried to convey that it was okay that Juliette hadn't emailed, that Marta wasn't going to hold it against her or pester her or do anything to make her feel uncomfortable. Maybe there would be a chance to say some of that out loud after the workshop. Or maybe it would be better to keep her distance—*show* that she meant no harm.

"We've been talking of God's love and forgiveness," said Kathy, after welcoming everyone and introducing the newcomer, Dianna, a yoga instructor. "Let's start tonight with one of Julian's famous passages. I'll read it out loud and then ask for your reactions." Kathy pulled her ragged copy of *Revelations of Divine Love* from the chair beside her and began: "'He shewed me a little thing, the quantity of a hazelnut, in the palm of my hand; and it was as round as a ball. I looked thereupon with eye of my understanding, and thought: *What may this be?* And it was answered generally thus: *It is all that is made.* I marvelled how it might last, for methought it might suddenly have fallen to naught for little. And I was answered in my understanding: *It lasteth, and ever shall for that God loveth it.* And so All-thing hath the Being by the love of God.'"

Marta considered the passage. How difficult yet comforting to consider the world as something that could be literally held in a loving hand.

"It's like Horton," said Adrian. "You know—*Horton Hears a Who!*"

"Maybe," Kathy said. Marta felt irritated. Couldn't they stick to the sacred for one second? But Kathy looked amused. "Although I'd much rather be in God's care than on a bumbling elephant's foot."

"It turned out all right." That was from Juliette.

"Yes. 'All shall be well,' perhaps. I think Dr. Seuss thought people could make a difference, could work toward making things well. But let's move on."

Kathy picked up another book, this one less worn. "I'm going to paraphrase Julian's thoughts, using a quotation from a book called *Enfolded in Love: Some of us believe that God is all powerful and may do everything; and that he is all wise and can do everything; but as for believing that he is all love and will do everything, there we hold back . . .*" Kathy looked up and made eye contact with Marta at that moment. "*Nothing hinders us more than the failure to understand this.*"

The ideas were moving too fast. Marta wanted to pause the lecture. If she were like Adrian, who had no qualms about interrupting, she would have asked Kathy to stop for a minute, or to repeat herself, just so that Marta could grasp the profundity of the words.

"We have a hard time believing that God can actually forgive the sins of our past. But Julian shows us that God is not an angry God." Kathy reached for her *Revelations of Divine Love* again. "*For I saw no whit of anger in God in short or in long term.*" She turned to another page. "*God is that goodness which cannot be angry for God is nothing but goodness.*" Kathy paused and looked around at the rapt faces. "So if you are not feeling God's love," Kathy went on, "it is not because the love is not there. Robert Llewelyn in his book *All Shall Be Well* uses an analogy of the sun. The sun is shining, and if you can't feel its warmth, maybe that's because you have an umbrella up. God looks upon us with pity and divine love, not blame, says Julian."

WHEN THE meeting ended, Marta rose to leave. "Marta." It was Juliette. "Sorry I didn't email you. I meant to, but I just seem to have such a hard time getting to things lately."

"No problem. I hope you didn't feel like I was prying or something." Marta tucked an erratic strand of hair behind her ear. Juliette's hair was pulled tight into a droopy bun at the top of her head. She wore no makeup. Not only the bun drooped; her eyes looked sunken, her shoulders slumped. She'd probably been gorgeous in her teens and twenties, Marta thought. The blond hair, the green eyes, the wide cheek bones. Maybe still was until the accident. She glanced at the little diamond and the thin platinum wedding band on Juliette's finger and wondered how supportive Juliette's spouse was of her suffering.

"Not at all. Hey, I don't drink at the moment—I'm on some medication—but do you want to grab a coffee or something? I mean, if you don't have other plans?"

"Sure. I'd love to. There are a few places around the corner on Dundas."

They walked along Dundas West. Marta stayed silent en route—everything she wanted to say, to ask, seemed nosy, too intimate to ask someone she'd just met. She felt awkward, but Juliette seemed too preoccupied, maybe too self-absorbed, to notice. "Does this look okay to you?" Marta motioned to the door of the Black Dice Café.

"Yeah, great."

They settled themselves at a Formica table. Juliette ordered a Diet Coke, and Marta did too, though really she wanted a rum and Coke. She found that the emotions she'd been experiencing weren't coming and going; rather they were accumulating. The wonder and the sense of joy she'd felt when Kathy spoke of God's forgiving love was still there, along with a little disbelief. She wanted to think some more about Dame Julian's words. The shame and relief after the arrest—they were present too and near the surface. And now, the awkwardness of this encounter and nervousness. What she needed was a long walk in the cool evening air. Or a long walk underground, although she wouldn't be risking that again. She added regret and sorrow to the emotional tapestry. "So," she said, straightening her back, "how do you spend your time?"

"I'm not sure." Juliette picked up the slice of lime on the edge of her glass and dropped it in. She kept her eyes on the glass as she spoke. "For the first couple of months I was a little obsessed with it all—with the jumper. I read the papers a lot. I searched through news reports, trolled the Internet looking for everything I could find about him. He was a teacher, and he was under investigation. A pedophile—or a suspected pedophile, I guess. We'll never know for sure now. His court case was coming up when he jumped in front of my train."

"And now? What do you do now?" Marta leaned forward so that she would not have to yell. Despite its name, the Black Dice Café was a bar, not a café, and the four occupants of the table next to them sounded like they had had several drinks each already.

"Well, I have two kids. My sister moved in with us after the— the accident. She's been looking after the house and the kids. My husband hates having her there, but I don't know what else to do. I actually don't do much. I don't sleep a lot, so I'm tired all the time. I'm on sick leave."

"Is the therapy helping?"

"I guess so." Her words were tentative. "My therapist claims it will get less terrifying with time. She makes me tell the story over and over again—maybe three times in a session, a few times a week. And over time it's supposed to become less of a horror and more of a scary story, just a scary story that happened to happen to me."

"But do you feel responsible?" Marta had no business asking that question, she knew.

"No." Juliette sounded abrupt. She spoke loudly; Marta no longer had to strain to hear her over the din of conversation, laughter, and a rock song she couldn't identify. "It could have been anyone. His timing was arbitrary. I just happened to be driving that train at the time that he worked up the courage or felt the most despair—whatever it was that made him jump. It wasn't me." The words sounded memorized; they rang with the strength of some-one else's conviction.

Marta raised her glass to her mouth and said nothing. Juliette had not taken even a sip yet. She stared at the table. Marta waited, in territory she knew. Juliette was leaning slightly forward, both hands on the table, immobile. Marta watched them and added compassion to her emotional tapestry. Not a tapestry, she thought. More like a wobbly layer cake, precarious, unstable. She was in no shape to play therapist for Juliette. Yet she waited. If Juliette changed the subject, she'd follow her lead. But if she wanted to divulge the truth, Marta would receive it.

Juliette looked up. Her wrists remained on the table, but she raised her hands. Her expression held both defeat and anguish. "I think it *was* me. He looked at me—our eyes met just as he jumped. Like he had picked me—something about me made him do it or helped him to do it. Not only did I not pull the brake in time, but something about my expression, the look in my eyes, encouraged him to do it."

Marta opened her mouth to say, "That's ridiculous." Then she closed it again. She let a moment pass. "I know that train of thought," she said. "'If I had just done this, or not done that. Said this, not said that . . .' It's endless."

Juliette leaned forward, lifting her elbows to the table. "You know what I mean?" Her voice was eager.

"Yeah. I know."

"It was your high school boyfriend, right?"

"Yes." Marta tilted her chair back. She realized she hadn't considered that the confidences would need to go both ways, that there might be a price to pay for Juliette's information. "Ex-boyfriend. We'd broken up."

"Did he leave a note?"

"No."

Juliette nodded. Marta braced herself for the obvious conclusion that Juliette would draw and say out loud. But Juliette was absorbed with her own combat. "What do you think? Do you think it was my fault?"

"No. But it doesn't matter what I think. What matters is what you think. It sounds like your therapist is trying to get you to convince yourself that it just happened—the timing was arbitrary; it had nothing to do with you. But maybe you're never going to be able to believe that. Maybe you'll always wonder if you could have pulled the brake sooner, or—I don't know—looked at him with the eyes of Gandhi or Mother Teresa or Jesus himself, and the empathy and kindness on your face would have made him reconsider and miraculously regain his balance." Marta shook her head. Juliette's mouth curved almost into a smile. She took a sip of her pop. Marta took a breath. "I think maybe what Kathy was telling us tonight is more helpful—that forgiveness is there, if we want to accept it. It's only you who can't forgive you."

THE BREEZE was cool when Marta walked home a short while later. She wished she'd brought a sweater. She thought about what she'd learned from the evening. Surely there were bits of truth that would help her move forward, boost her up. It wasn't that she expected to be walking on air, but some new hope, some more clarity, some more purpose would be nice. She replayed Dame Julian's messages about God's love and his capacity for forgiveness. And

Juliette's story, the similarities between her own and Juliette's self-blame and emotional paralysis. Marta searched for comfort as she mulled over their conversation. But she realized that what she felt was jealousy. Jealousy because the suicide that touched Juliette had such clear purpose behind it. Whatever the man's complex reasons for jumping, whether logical or illogical, sane or sick, the public understanding was simple. It wasn't random or arbitrary. He was a suspected pedophile with a court case looming close. The pressure was too much. Even death by suicide had its continuum of tragedy, depending on how explicable the death was. A terminally ill cancer patient suffering terribly, and watching her family watch her suffer, takes a fatal overdose of a prescription medication. So sad. And yet, understandable. She couldn't bear the suffering anymore. The upstanding citizen who is caught with his hand in the cookie jar and now faces public humiliation and years of jail time to account for his actions. What a waste, people say, shaking their heads. But explicable. He was a coward as well as a fraud. A high school boy with his whole future ahead of him. Upstanding and intact family, no instability or mental illness in his past. No indications that there had been abuse of any sort, no signs of drug use, no problems at school, whether social or academic. No traumatic events that explained the sudden death—except for his girlfriend dumping him five months earlier. But surely that was a normal trauma; few teenagers escaped their adolescent years without heartbreak.

Marta's shoulders hunched up around her ears.

CHAPTER THIRTEEN

JENN'S LAUGHTER WHEN MARTA GOT to the part about sinking onto the sidewalk in handcuffs startled Marta. "It's not that funny."

"Well, it turned out all right, and it *is* funny. Not funny that you've been going into the drains, but hilarious that you got caught. And handcuffed. Wish I had a photo!" Jenn's laughter pealed again.

"Wow." Marta walked a few paces ahead of Jenn. The evening air was thick and sultry; it had been a steamy day, with high temperatures and humidity, too hot for exercise. "Do you think it's cool enough yet to go for a walk?" Marta had said when Jenn popped by around seven o'clock. It was the second week of August now, and days were beginning to shorten, the sun tilting lower in the sky. They strolled along Sylvan Avenue, a chorus of cicadas serenading them from the Norway maples lining the streets. "Hey, look at that!" Marta pointed to the right. Four houses in a row slanted in four different directions, not a true line among them. Marta squinted, trying to figure out which of the tall, narrow buildings was the straightest. She decided she'd need a level to be sure.

"Creeks underneath those houses?" The expression on Jenn's face was the mix of pleasure and curiosity that Marta knew well from their years of childhood explorations. She wondered if Jenn was secretly jealous of her underground journeys.

"No—I've read about this. They were built on ash landfill. Ash from the coal-burning fireplaces that all the houses in this neighbourhood had back then."

"*The fool-ish man built his house upon the sand, the fool-ish man built his house u-pon the sand . . .*" Jenn's voice rang out as she sang the old Sunday school song.

"Maybe," said Marta, still peering at the structures. "But they've stayed standing for ninety years and counting."

"I'd rather live in one of those." Jenn pointed at a sturdy Victorian detached house across the street.

"Yeah—that was built earlier. Then the air got smoky from all the coal they burned in the early 1900s—apparently it was like living in fog. And the streets were too narrow for cars, which were all the rage. So the middle-class people who lived in those houses"—she pointed to the Victorian—"moved north, and that's when all the cheaper, industrial houses were built. Infill houses built on landfill."

"How do you know all this stuff?"

"Remember two years ago when I was thinking of renting space somewhere in the neighbourhood to grow vegetables?" Jenn's expression made her laugh. "When we were little, I hated weeding the garden and picking peas and beans as much as you did, but now I miss it. Anyway, I was talking to a woman at the farmer's market in Dufferin Grove about it, and she told me, 'Don't do it—the soil's contaminated.' So I did some research. She's right: PAH contamination. I don't know what that is, but it's still from the coal. Doesn't sound good to eat."

"So why do you keep living in this neighbourhood?"

"I like it. I like the way it shows how the city developed. The history of it. The human face. There's something beautiful about how organic it is—that long curve in College Street because it was built to avoid the Garrison Creek Ravine. Or the really old houses on Shannon Street, that have two front facades—they face their backyards *and* the street."

"Why?"

"They're on the ravine. Garrison Creek."

"Is it true that the city buried bridges when they buried Garrison Creek?"

"I don't think so. The creek was already buried. They buried the bridges when they evened out the ravines. The Crawford Bridge and the Harbord Bridge."

"You should lead those history walks—you know, the weekend walks in historical neighbourhoods."

"Would anyone be interested in this neighbourhood? It's pretty shabby."

They walked a block along Lindsey Avenue, then turned the corner onto an even narrower street. "Look." Marta pointed, but she didn't have to—Jenn was already studying the 1920s duplex, which appeared to be on the brink of disaster. The two halves sagged backward and careened away from each other—they looked like reflections in a funhouse mirror.

"Betcha they have trouble hanging their artwork. Do you align it to the top of the sofa or the top of the wall?" Jenn sounded more amused than concerned.

"It'd be easy to find anything you dropped—it would just roll to the back corner."

"There's a contrast." Jenn pointed across the street at a squat brick 1950s house, its lines rectangular and true. She turned to look at Marta. "Cities would be so much neater if you planned one from start to finish and then didn't have to change things."

"That could only happen if technology never changed, or we never learned anything new."

"I suppose." The women resumed walking. "I was reading about geothermal heating. That they're going to have to dig up the roads to install the equipment needed—it's the only flat space big enough downtown." Jenn waved her hand to the south.

"And then there's the cables needed for Internet and phones," Marta said. "The problems of building a city over time—nothing's neatly planned out at the beginning."

"Kind of like a person."

Marta rolled her eyes at Jenn. "Don't get all psychological on me."

Jenn shrugged. "Just saying."

Marta shifted away from Jenn and walked in silence. The sunlight that slipped between houses was in layers now—pink, orange, red.

"What do you think Matt would do if I left him?" The words were abrupt.

Jenn looked startled, but recovered quickly. "Get a girlfriend."

"That's it?"

"What do you think he would do?" She sounded irritated. "Pound at your door? Send you twelve thousand text messages a day begging you to come back to him?"

"Probably not. But you don't think he'd . . . get depressed?"

Jenn came to a complete stop. She faced Marta, and Marta watched her eyes widen. "Oh." She took Marta's hand. "Oh. You think—you think—no. I don't think he's unstable in that way. Matt takes care of himself—he's really good at taking care of himself."

"You're biased. You've never liked him."

"That's true. But I still think he'd be fine if you left him."

"Do you remember that rock that Benny gave us?"

"Our cousin Benny?"

"Yeah."

"What rock?"

"When I was about eight. He said it was radioactive. It was just an ordinary rock—I think it had some fool's gold in it. Pyrite. He said he got it at a mine. Told me that if I put it in the fish tank, all the fish would die. I didn't believe him."

Jenn exhaled. "That's what killed the fish? Mom wouldn't tell me."

"I did it."

"That's silly—how would he have gotten a radioactive rock?"

"Maybe not radioactive. But toxic."

"Why are you telling me this?"

"No reason. I was just thinking about it." Marta hummed as she walked, hummed her own song, changing a word or two. "*Your love is the grass I'm about to cut, while I watch you and pray for your feet.*" She realized that changing "you're" to "I'm" in that line made the rest of the line confusing. Why would someone's feet need praying for if that someone wasn't the one operating the lawnmower? She needed to throw out this song.

"Mr. Maas hasn't phoned back."

"Maybe he's not going to. Someone who was able to hold on to a letter for thirteen years without peeking is someone who's pretty good at not taking action."

"I suppose. Why do you think he never got married?"

"Because he's gay."

"Yeah, that's what I thought. I wouldn't want to be gay in that community. Wonder why he stayed."

"Have you ever wondered . . ." Jenn's voice trailed off.

"What?"

"Whether Aaron was gay? Whether that's why he killed himself?"

Marta gazed at another tilting house, imagining walking the crooked floors in the dark or while tipsy. "I've considered most reasons by now."

"I remember talking to Dad about it—it was when I came home for Easter one year when I was in university. I knew you blamed yourself, and it made me feel bad. Helpless."

"It's not just me; other people blame me too."

"Yeah. That's what I talked to Dad about. Asked him how people could be so cruel. I was taking a psychology course about theories of human behaviour, and none of them seemed to explain that to me—why people blamed you."

"So what did Dad say?" She realized that it was more than idle curiosity that prompted that question. Years ago, she had rejected her dad's plentiful attempts at comfort. How could he console her when he denied her contribution to the outcome, her sin of omission?

"Dad said that everyone seeks reasons—we long for reasons —to explain terrible events. We want to blame someone, or even ourselves"—Jenn paused—"because it feels easier to live with guilt or blame than with uncertainty and a lack of closure."

From the corner of her eye, Marta saw Jenn peering at her. She kept her eyes on the sidewalk far ahead. "Trust me, guilt isn't easy."

"Yeah, I can tell. Maybe Dad was right, though. I'd already thought of explanations for Aaron's death—was he bullied, was he gay, did he have schizophrenia?"

The questions were rhetorical, but Marta answered anyway. "Maybe he became depressed—I don't know. If there were warning signs, I didn't catch them. Even in retrospect, I can't see them, except for the noose on his pencil case, maybe. Maybe he changed a lot after we moved. I wish I knew that. Maybe he fell into depression. And no one caught it. Maybe there were signs, but they were too subtle. I don't know. I wasn't there."

"Maybe he was experimenting sexually? Do you know what I mean?"

"Auto-erotic asphyxiation. I've thought of that too." Marta turned away from Jenn to hide a sudden flush. Of all the theories, she found this one the most disturbing. Mortifying, really. She was his *girlfriend*. Or had been.

"So why do you keep blaming yourself?"

Marta shrugged.

"Dad said sometimes bad things happen that have no logic, no explanation. He said there are moments when it seems like things are not even in God's hands. Maybe Aaron's life wasn't in your hands."

"Mmm."

"Maybe you should talk to Dad about it."

Marta's eyebrows inched up. "Mom and Dad and I don't have those kinds of conversations anymore. We chit-chat. When I was there the May long weekend—three months ago?—we talked about books and movies and their health and the fact that you had broken up with yet another boyfriend. Oh, and my work."

"They worry about me too much. I just haven't met the right guy."

Marta's eyebrows rose again. "You're the classic guy who can't commit, only you're a woman."

"I just need to meet the right person. But don't change the subject. You should talk to Mom and Dad."

"Nah. They don't approve of Matt, and I know what they'd say about Aaron. We've had that conversation."

"What would they say?"

"That it's time to move on. Let go. Accept his death. 'Accept your life,' I think Dad said, last time we talked about it."

"When was that?"

"Eleven or twelve years ago."

Now Jenn's eyebrows flew up, but she dropped the subject. "Look at this." She stopped to examine the rows of corn someone had planted in a front yard the size of Marta's living room. Marta stepped beside her and fingered the still-green silk on an ear near the fence. Then Jenn said, "Are you going to go back down in the sewers?"

"Not any time soon." Marta let go of the corn. She hoped it

ripened in time, that mischievous kids didn't tamper with the crop, that insects or birds didn't enjoy the bounty before the gardener could. What a commitment to dedicate your entire front yard, small though it was, in the hopes of gaining a few ears of corn. "Oliver sent me an email checking to see if I was okay. He's going to wait a month or two before doing any more exploration himself. The arrest won't stop him, though—nothing stops him. He was born for trouble."

"And you?"

"I have no idea what I was born for. Not singing or writing songs—I'm sure of that lately."

"I like your songs."

"That's because you're my sister. My songs suck."

"You're too hard on yourself."

"Maybe."

They looped northeast to Bloor and Shaw. "I'm going to walk to Christie and grab the subway home," said Jenn.

"Okay. See you soon."

Abruptly Jenn put her arm around Marta. "Take care."

"I will. I do."

Marta trod west along Bloor. It was not a pretty stretch—dilapidated storefronts lined the street. They dated from the early part of the twentieth century, and even then it was a working-class area of town. At Bloor and Dovercourt she paused before turning south to her home. She peered around her, seeking a sign. Or at least seeking the meaning of the signs she had received. Kathy had said it took Julian of Norwich years and years to work out the meaning of her visions. Perhaps Marta was rushing things. She gazed at the jumble around her, the Mini Mart, a Jamaican patty restaurant, a cheap furniture shop, a coin laundry, an office offering to fight traffic tickets, a tired-looking pizza place. Dusk had fallen to dark, turning the shabbiness shadowy in spite of the streetlights. She felt disheartened by the grimness, the poverty, the detritus. This was a neighbourhood of flotsam and jetsam. Rubble. People clinging to odd businesses, peeling paint, crumbling brick. Maybe she should move to a different neighbourhood. Teach at a different school.

There was a high school in Etobicoke that was advertising for a guidance counsellor. Near Royal York and Bloor, a chic neighbourhood with elegant houses—all clean brick faces, tidy shrubbery, window boxes bursting with geraniums and trailing ivy, wrought-iron gates leading to manicured yards that she imagined as tranquil oases of flagstone, boxwood, and perennial grasses. The teens who lived in those houses would probably be different. They might have more drive, a greater sense of future. Their parents had money; they spoke fluent English. Gave their kids piano and violin lessons, put them in French immersion, took them on vacations.

But who would look after her kids, last names *K* through *N*?

You're not irreplaceable, she told herself. And there were people far more capable than she was. People who were confident in their convictions, who cleared through problems like bulldozers moving debris. She was mousy as a guidance counsellor, good with kids going through trauma, kind to troublemakers, a bit of a pushover. Really, how much good was she doing? She looked around again at the dark. But it wasn't that dark. Artificial light from streetlamps, stoplights, and storefronts pulsed. She addressed God. "*You sent me signs, but I don't know what they mean. Help.*" She sent the prayer out like she was launching a message in a bottle, imagining it sailing outward. In the distance, she heard the scream of a siren—a fire engine, she thought. A sign from God that help was coming, or a reminder that others were in more dire need than she was?

Marta trudged home.

LATER, WHEN she examined what possessed her to return to Lethbridge, she concluded that the cockroaches were the instrument of change. Like first raindrops, they were a shift in the weather that heaved her into action. She thought she saw something scuttle when she turned on the light in the kitchen. A June bug, she told herself, or maybe a cricket, although she heard no chirping. But the next night she stayed up late to finish her essay. Matt had been right—her topic was too broad and there were few certain conclusions she could make, only suggestions. She tried narrowing the topic, focusing only on English as a Second Language. Still too broad but better. She had much to learn as a guidance counsellor—there were many ways yet to grow and explore. Probably she could work a lifetime and still not be an expert. Was that depressing or exhilarating? she wondered. Maybe it just depended on how much sleep you'd had. She felt exhausted. Matt had been in bed for a couple of hours, saying a rather terse goodnight to her before vanishing to their bedroom. The distance between them these days was a city block—he disapproving, she defensive, aloof, and cool.

She closed down the computer—she'd print the paper tomorrow and deliver it to her professor. Feeling parched, she marched into the kitchen and opened the fridge. The glow of the light from the open door illuminated the wall and counter. And she spotted two cockroaches—a large one at eye level on the tile above the sink, flat against it, like a wall ornament. It was glossy brown, the shape of a giant manicured fingernail. Six hairy legs and two long feelers wriggling like tiny snakes. She felt sick. And a smaller one on the counter, scuttling into the crevice beside the stove as she watched. She needed to kill the one on the wall, yet the thought revolted her, the way it would crunch. Smear the wall. Or it would get away, and she'd feel the horror of knowing it was somewhere in the house. It and a hundred more like it, probably.

Matt. She would wake him up.

She walked into the bedroom and put a hand on his shoulder. "Please come to the kitchen," she said.

She was sure he'd been asleep, but he responded to the distress in her voice and rose quickly.

"We have a problem." She tried to keep the hysteria out of her voice. Really. They were just insects. Not poisonous snakes or a cougar or a burglar.

He followed her, wearing only his boxers. She avoided turning on the kitchen light, not wanting it to spook the bug on the wall. Instead she opened the fridge again, letting its glow light the wall. The roach was still there. "I saw another on the counter. I saw one last night too, but I didn't know it was a cockroach till I saw these tonight." She heard the horror in her tone.

"And this couldn't wait till morning?" Matt sounded irritated.

"Well, we need to kill it. I just needed help killing it."

"Got a bleeding heart for bugs now too?"

"No! Don't be a jerk. I'm creeped out by the bugs. I just couldn't smush it."

"Yet you can walk through sewers." Matt curled his hand into a fist and smashed it against the wall. The flattened bug slid to the floor, leaving the smear Marta expected. She shuddered.

"There." Matt walked to the sink and turned on the water, rinsed his hand. Dried it on the dish towel. Marta made a note to put the towel in the laundry the next morning. "Happy?"

"No. Of course I'm not happy. Thank you for getting up and killing that bug. I'm happy about that. But we have a cockroach infestation. We have to do something."

"A few bugs is hardly an *infestation*." He emphasized the word as if it were ridiculous.

"If you see one, you have a hundred more."

"Okay, fine. We'll get some spray or chalk."

"How do you think we got them?" They kept their floors and counters clean; they stored their food in sealed containers.

"Marta, they're everywhere. Could have been in a cardboard box from No Frills. Could have come in from the neighbours. Could even have come home in your school bag."

Marta wrapped her arms around herself. "I think we should hire an exterminator."

"Fine. Do what you want. I might not be living here much longer anyway."

Marta's stomach, already agitated from the cockroaches, heaved. She felt sucker-punched—although she had never been sucker-punched, or punched at all for that matter. He was jumping off the teeter-totter, abandoning her as it plunged to the ground. Though she had been contemplating leaving Matt just a day before, she wanted to clutch his arms, beg him to stay. "What does that mean?"

"Well, you don't want me—you've made that perfectly clear." He looked defiant and defeated at the same time.

"I—I *love* you." It was true, she thought, as she looked at him standing in his grey boxers in the bug-infested kitchen. She did love him. If only she knew how to get love back.

"I love *you*," he said and shrugged. His tone was matter of fact, like the statement was self-evident but unimportant.

They stood in silence, Marta watching Matt, Matt staring at the drain in the sink. "I think I have to go to Lethbridge," Marta said. Her stomach hurt.

Matt's gaze swivelled, and he looked into her eyes. He nodded slowly. "Okay. Want me to come along?"

Marta found herself nodding with him. But she said, "We can't afford two flights. We can't really afford one. My course this summer cost almost seven hundred dollars."

"If you need to go, you should go."

Marta nodded again. "Okay."

CHAPTER FOURTEEN

THE FLIGHT FROM TORONTO TO Calgary was pleasant—Marta watched a romantic comedy with the right combination of predictability and charm to numb her fear and dull the misgivings. But on the commuter flight to Lethbridge, her anxiety rose so high she could not stop herself from fidgeting. There was nothing to decide—once a plane took off you were committed to the destination. Yet Marta's fingers skittered in her palm. She supposed she could just stay the two nights she had reserved in the hotel, watch a lot of TV, return home. Make noncommittal noises when Matt and Jenn asked her about the trip. But Jenn would press for details. *And* Jenn had announced to their parents that Marta was travelling to Lethbridge, so they would demand a report. They had phoned before she left Toronto—before Marta was aware that they knew of her plans. It felt like a curveball when she didn't know she was up to bat. Her mother first. "What are you doing, Marta?"

"Emptying the dishwasher."

"You know what I mean. Why are you going to Lethbridge? Why now? Why at all?"

"I—don't know. I was talking to Mr. Maas, and I think I need to go there and talk to some people."

"What do you hope to achieve?" Her mother's voice was

concerned but tired. The way the therapist had sounded all those years ago. A bit exasperated.

"Nothing, Mom. I just want to be there. Talk to Mr. Maas."

"Are you visiting Aaron's parents?"

"I don't know."

Her mother had passed the phone to her dad. "Honey," he said without preamble, "that family has its own agenda and its own demons. He was their only child. Protect yourself. Don't buy into their view of things. You can't imagine their hurt or their guilt, and so you can't imagine what they have had to do to live with Aaron's death. For them, the choice was to blame themselves or to blame you. They didn't see another way. There was no talking to them. Better if you didn't go there at all." He spoke without pausing, and Marta heard not only the words, but also the tone, read it the way she, like all children, she supposed, read their parents, perceiving all the love and the fear behind the speeches.

"I have to, Dad."

"Then God go with you."

MARTA HAD accepted the *Calgary Herald* that the flight attendant handed her on her way into the plane, and now she looked up her horoscope. It wasn't that she believed in the zodiac—she shrugged when people asked her what sign she was. Yet she habitually sought out her forecast in newspapers and magazines. She justified her behaviour by telling herself that God could, if he chose to, use horoscopes to send someone a message.

Make a new friend or work connection today—your social energy needs exercise. You may find it easier than usual to say hello to that cute stranger, too, so go for it!

Maybe not.

The "Today's Your Birthday" horoscope caught her eye, although her birthday was three months away. *More important than what you know or what you don't know is what you don't want to know. This is what you need to contemplate right now.* Not very cheery for a birthday, Marta thought. This could possibly apply to her situation, though. Might be worth considering in more depth. Since she thought astrology was bogus, why feel tied to her own sign? No, it wasn't her birthday. Not even close. She closed the paper.

The connection in Calgary had been quick, and, with the two-hour time difference from Toronto, Marta arrived at her hotel with most of the afternoon still ahead. She hung up a blouse and a jacket, then went outside. The wind was hot and dry on her face, a welcome contrast to the moist, sticky heat she'd left in Toronto. She studied the landscape. This area had not been as developed when Marta lived here as a child, so it felt strange to her—or perhaps strangely familiar, looking like every other North American city, with its generic row of hotels and fast food restaurants. She walked along Mayor Magrath Drive, noting the food choices—pizza, hamburgers, Chinese, steak, donairs. Right now, the nervousness was a fist in her stomach, but if she ever felt hungry again, she'd have a decision to make. Her fingers twitched in her clammy palm.

She strode back to the hotel. She should just call Mr. Maas—get a move on, as her mother would say. They'd had a voice mail exchange before she left, Mr. Maas's message inviting her to drop by at teatime on one of the days she was in town. The notion had struck her as quaint. A bit nostalgic. Teatime was lost to her now. But it had been a part of every childhood weekend and holiday. When she visited a farm friend, the men and boys came in from the barn or the fields in the mid-afternoon, and everyone gathered around the kitchen table. There was tea, cookies, and squares. *Koek*—the Dutch honey cake that now she had only when she visited her parents. Toast and Gouda cheese if you wanted a sandwich. Reports on the afternoon's labour so far; gossip about people they knew. All her childhood friends had been Dutch in background, and their families associated mainly with one another and other Dutch families. This led to oddnesses such as knowing one's next-door neighbours only well enough to nod to, but knowing intimate details about people many kilometres away if they happened to have come from Holland. She had tried once to describe the community to Matt, whose background was British—enough generations back that he felt little, if any, cultural affinity to other English immigrants. "You have to understand," she told Matt, "that they not only socialized with other Dutch immigrant families but also banked at the Dutch Canadian Credit Union, bought food at The Wooden Shoe or Koster's Deli, and used the advertising pages in the church directory to find Dutch Canadian real estate agents, lawyers, insurance companies." At the Covenant Christian Reformed Church, the Calvin Christian High School, where Marta attended, and the Calvin Christian Elementary School, where Jenn was still a student when they moved to Ontario, almost all the families were Dutch Canadian. The school's culture was insular but academic, with biblical studies integrated into the curriculum for all the classes.

"Was your school like a cult?" Matt had asked.

"Not at all. It was a little conservative, maybe—we couldn't wear midriff-baring T-shirts or have body piercings other than ear piercings. But it wasn't preachy or anything. The teachers were geeky, but so were public school teachers. We did some cool things too, like a couple of days when I was in grade ten, we had all these guest speakers and did workshops and simulations to learn about world hunger. And in grade eleven we did a big fundraiser for victims of the Red River Flood." It had been, in retrospect, a solid school that provided a sound education. And while they perhaps weren't halcyon days—Marta was thin and shy and too serious by teenage standards to be a desirable friend—they were safe. Predictable and comfortable. She did well in her classes, especially social science and music. It was a fine community for those who fit in, and Marta did. Had.

Mr. Maas's house was a tidy, stuccoed split-level not far from the Christian high school campus. Close enough that Marta felt uneasy. She thought about Juliette and her fear of subway stations. If Juliette could go back into a subway station, surely Marta could revisit the neighbourhoods that held echoes of her and Aaron's past.

Mr. Maas—Henry, as he had identified himself on her voice mail—opened the door wide. He welcomed her in that warm, hearty tone Marta recognized as the one teachers use to put students at ease. A tone she herself used. She felt grateful. "You look more mature, but otherwise you haven't changed a bit. I would have recognized you anywhere!"

Mr. Maas looked the same too. He must have aged—they were both thirteen years older. But she'd thought of him as old when he taught her—he must have been in his mid- or late-forties—and now he still looked middle-aged. Greying hair, balding at the temples, glasses with brown frames that butted against shaggy eyebrows. Eyes that were intelligent and kind. Thin elbows that seemed to move of their own accord. She remembered that they used to make fun of his odd, jerky arm movements, and felt guilty.

"Come, sit down. I'm going to bring in a pot of tea and some goodies. I didn't bake, but I visited The Wooden Shoe this morning and got some currant buns and boterkoek."

"That sounds good." She could manage some tea, she thought, taking a seat on the beige sofa. But not the goodies, not even boterkoek. It was a rare treat for her—you had to bake it yourself or go to the Holland Store way out on Weston Road to find it in Toronto. But she just wanted the news, the letter. Or maybe she didn't want to open it. It lay in front of her on the coffee table. Aaron's handwriting—more familiar-looking than her own high school handwriting had appeared on the letter she received—raised the hair on her arms. That's what happened with death. Other people's lives moved on; they developed and changed. Even their handwriting grew older. This was an artefact, a fossil. She wrapped her arms around herself. She thought of Juliette again, and told herself she could manage to stay calm. Look at something else. She tried surveying the living room for signs of Mr. Maas's sexual orientation. There was nothing obvious. Or at least nothing stereotypical—no effeminate touches like trinkets, no fussy decorating scheme, no high-end, better-taste-than-most furniture. The armchairs were beige plaid in a matched set—from the Sears catalogue, by the looks of them. A William Kurelek painting hung over the sofa and a winter scene of the Rockies over the south wall. Lots of plants—Mr. Maas had a green thumb. The orchids were blooming in profusion.

Mr. Maas—Henry—walked in. "Can I pour you some tea?"

"Yes, please."

"Oh—do you take sugar?"

"No, thanks." She did, but he hadn't brought it, and sugar seemed trivial right now. The approach-avoidance bop going on in her head absorbed all her attention.

"You're well?"

"Yes, thank you. And you?"

"Things are fine with me. Actually, I think we had this conversation on the phone." His smile was wry, but she could see the nervousness in the upright posture, the stiff arms as he stirred milk into his tea. He regarded her, then the letter. "You've come a long way for this. I guess we should open it." His voice jovial, his expression uneasy.

"Yes, please. I'm going to visit Aaron's parents too. If the letter is—" *the word* benign came to mind, but she didn't want to say it out loud since it would make them consider the opposite possibility, that the letter was malignant. That indeed something must have been malignant to make Aaron hang himself from a light fixture that September night. Now that she was in Lethbridge, the memories were not only closer, they were more visceral. She visualized the Woudas' house, Aaron's room, and Aaron, swinging from the noose he had knotted. She had picked her teacup up, but she placed it back on the table. "If it's something that will bring them comfort, maybe I can take it with me."

Mr. Maas looked at her skeptically. "I can see why you want to read this letter, but I can't see why you want to visit the Woudas. It's a bad idea. They don't appear to have—healed—very much since he died."

"What do you mean?"

"I mean, they haven't recovered. They may still be in shock. You could be walking into the lion's den."

That brought to mind Daniel, the biblical Daniel. Maybe she'd be okay, even if they were lionlike.

Mr. Maas picked up the envelope. He turned it over, then turned it face up. Turned it over again. "Here goes." He tore it open with his thumb and finger. He handed the letter to Marta, who took it reverently, as if it were a relic newly unearthed from a sepulchre.

"Shall I read out loud?"

He nodded at her, though his eyes, she thought, were saying no.

Dear self,
This assignment is retarded. Why would I give a shit thirteen years from now about what I thought in high school? Hopefully by then I'll be miles away

from here. Somewhere where sunflowers don't grow.
Fucking sunflowers.

Marta glanced at Mr. Maas after the curse and tried not to wince.
Students got sent to the principal for using that word in earshot of a
teacher when she was in school.
She looked back down.

What the hell—here goes. In thirteen years, I plan to
be rich, famous, and somewhere else.

What I wouldn't give to find a soulmate
Someone else to catch this drift
And what I wouldn't give to meet a kindred
Enough about me, let's talk about you for a
    minute
Enough about you, let's talk about life for a while
The conflicts, the craziness, and the sound of
    pretenses
Falling all around . . . all around
Why are you so petrified of silence
Here can you handle this?

All I really want is some peace man
A place to find a common ground
And all I really want is a wavelength
All I really want is some comfort

A way to get my hands untied
And all I really want is some justice.

At the bottom, he had signed his name. Marta folded the letter in two and looked up at Mr. Maas, who had crossed his leg over his knee and was stroking his chin, his elbows out to the sides.

"Did he write that poem, do you think?"

Marta reached for the envelope and slid the letter back inside. "It's not a poem. They're lyrics. Alanis Morissette. He really liked her music. Had a poster of her in his room. Played that cd over and over in his car."

"Was it angry music?"

Marta thought. They had been teenagers. They hadn't perceived Alanis as being angry. A bit of a badass, maybe. Bold and honest. But she could be sweet and romantic too. Insightful.

She shrugged. She felt deflated. The letter was unhappy. But she knew Aaron was unhappy. It was just a few weeks after she'd broken up with him. He was dreading the summer—hating working for his dad on the farm. The letter told her nothing she didn't already know.

"Did he change after I left, do you know? Did he—seem depressed that September?"

Mr. Maas gave a slight shrug, then nodded. "We had a team of grief counsellors into the school after he died. They talked to the staff and his friends—and any of his classmates who wanted to see them. He'd worked long hours that summer—they were installing a new irrigation system. No one had seen much of him.

Brian Haagstra—who led the Youth Group at church, remember?—said he hadn't shown up at any events. His buddies—who were they again?"

"Dylan Verstrait and Paul Mercer were his closest friends."

"Yeah, I remember. We were told to keep a close eye on them because sometimes with suicides—well, you're a guidance counsellor—you know."

Copycat deaths. Marta remembered how bleak she had felt when the news came. She folded her hands.

"Did they say anything?"

"Not to me. I heard from Christine Vanderpool that Paul said Aaron wasn't the same that fall. Moped around, didn't want to hang around with them. But Paul told Christine that he had no idea Aaron was suicidal."

This was a part of the community Marta felt glad to have escaped. Christine Vanderpool had been the only guidance counsellor at Calvin High, and everybody knew she was a huge gossip. Divulge any secrets to her and the whole staff would know. Then she'd pass the news on to her friends on the Willing Workers committee at church, and almost before you got your words out in her office, the entire Dutch Christian community would know your business.

Mr. Maas picked up the letter and held it as if it were a wriggling worm. He shook his head from side to side, slowly and deliberately. "I don't think this letter is going to do his parents any good." He spoke as if this needed saying, and Marta smiled. Henry Maas smiled back. The smile turned to laughter, and for a moment, the anxiety and the sadness abated, and she and Henry both laughed.

CHAPTER FIFTEEN

MARTA STEELED HERSELF AGAINST SECOND thoughts when she arrived back at the hotel, nudging aside qualms and misgivings, turning her back on the warnings she'd received. She still knew the number by heart. Neither she nor Aaron—nor any of their friends—had cellphones in high school, so they relied on landlines. It had always been nerve-wracking to call his house, forging through the awkward moment of identifying herself to the parent who answered, navigating the uneasy exchange of small talk. She recalled the relief she would experience when Aaron picked up the phone and told her he was on his way to his room to talk to her from there.

Receiver in hand, she reviewed her strategies. She hoped it was Mr. Wouda who answered. She had considered her opening line, their possible responses, her replies. She'd tried to predict the varied pathways that the conversation could take, to calculate the likely outcomes. It had taken her hours, days to plan the call.

It took two minutes to execute, and her armpits were soaked when she hung up.

"You're here in Coaldale?" It was Mr. Wouda.

"Well, in Lethbridge. I could be there in forty-five minutes, and I won't stay long. Just a minute of your time. Maybe after supper tonight? Or sometime tomorrow?" She sounded as timid and tentative as she had as a teenaged girl.

She drove east along Crowsnest Trail toward Coaldale. The fields were in bloom, thousands of smiling golden faces. A breeze made the sunflowers ripple and bob, and she felt encouraged, though she stopped short of believing the nodding heads to be a sign.

The exterior of the house gave no indication of the blight that had befallen the family. It was an ordinary ranch-style home with white siding and grey shutters, the appearance tidy and neutral. But the interior of the house was even more grim than she remembered it. Brown seemed the dominant colour: dark hardwood floors, a sombre walnut-stained wall unit, coffee tables in a hue that was lighter but still subdued. Mr. Wouda had let her in, and now he motioned her to the taupe leather sofa, facing the view of the sunset glowing across the prairie.

Mrs. Wouda entered the room. She avoided Marta's eyes. "The sun shines right on your face in this room," she said. She jerked the wooden blinds shut. She settled herself in a small, stiff armchair, the seat farthest from Marta. Mr. Wouda perched on the edge of a La-Z-Boy. He cleared his throat and arranged his face in what Marta decided to believe was polite welcome. She wedged herself closer to the arm of the sofa.

"How have you been?" asked Mr. Wouda.

"Uh—fine. I'm living in Toronto. I did music for a while"— that was an overstatement—"and now I'm working at a school." She avoided saying both "guidance counsellor" and "high school."

Mr. Wouda nodded, and then silence ensued. Marta glanced at Mrs. Wouda. She had an urban look about her—sleek capris, a tailored blouse, ballet flats, her hair in a neat low ponytail, pearls in her earlobes. She was tall and slim, with the kind of posture that made you straighten your own spine when you looked at her. It was only her face that gave away her age. How old was she? Marta wondered. In her late fifties, maybe? She looked old, her face grooved, the skin sallow. Grief, Marta thought, sped up aging probably more than exposure to sun. That made her notice Mrs. Wouda's pale complexion. It was nearly the end of August, yet Mrs. Wouda had vampire skin. Maybe she never left the house. Marta had the feeling she was in a tomb, a fortress shut against all light—the sun, the sunflowers, anything that might provide joy.

She looked at Mr. Wouda. When she first met him, the Woudas had been in Canada only six or seven years. He now wore the weather-beaten face of all the area farmers, a face that endured extremes—below-freezing temperatures, sizzling sun, sleet, wind. Mostly the wind. It came in breezes, gusts, blasts, and squalls. In the summer it spread grass fires; it prompted fierce thunderstorms and sometimes tornados. In the winter, it whipped falling snow into blizzards that tore down trees and wires. Marta could not tell whether Mr. Wouda's scoured face was the result of living in the aftermath of trauma or just of living in the elements.

"Well, I won't keep you. I guess I just wanted to say . . ." Her voice faltered. Who all had told her that this was a bad idea? Jenn, Mr. Maas. Matt—although he had come around. Her parents. She inhaled. "I just want to say that I'm sorry. About Aaron. I'm sorry he died. And I'm sorry that I missed the signs that he was, that he was . . ." She had memorized the speech but couldn't recall it.

Not with the way Mr. Wouda's carriage was changing as she spoke. He was sagging, the sinewy muscles and working man's shoulders turning lumpish. "Well, I'm sorry."

Mr. Wouda's hand travelled to his forehead. For a moment his face looked open and vulnerable, but then it shifted, despair closing over the naked emotion like a tarp. His arm fell back to his lap, and he stared at the floor. Mrs. Wouda considered him, her mouth in a tight line. Then she seemed to rouse herself. She sat even more upright and leaned forward. "Well, thank you for coming, Marta." The Dutch accent that made the old-timers—the immigrants who came in the 1950s—seem old-fashioned, made Mrs. Wouda sound sophisticated and cosmopolitan. Or maybe it was the carefully correct grammar, the precise enunciation. "I hope that you have some other business here in Alberta, though, because coming all this way to tell us you are sorry seems a waste of time. Your being sorry will not return our son, will it?"

"Now, Anneke," said Mr. Wouda. His voice was tired and impotent.

Marta flinched. She looked down. It's okay, she told herself. She breathed a slow, deliberate breath. The coffee table had a shelf underneath. A stack of books was piled biggest to smallest, the spines in a flawless line. Mrs. Wouda would have trouble living in one of the crooked Toronto houses, Marta thought. The cover of the top book sported a peregrine falcon. A Lone Pine Field Guide titled *Birds of Alberta*. The falcons were endangered, driven to the edge of extinction by pesticide use, especially DDT. Until recently they had been very rare in Ontario. There had been an article in the *Toronto Star* in July. The birds were hapless parents, their carelessness contributing to an eighty percent infant mortality rate, or something like that. Marta remembered reading about volunteer groups—they set up nest boxes on the ledge of the Toronto Sheraton for a pair, after the mother falcon rolled her first egg off the ledge. The volunteers banded babies, even installed transmitters on the little ones for satellite tracking. And it was working—the falcons were making a comeback.

Marta dragged her eyes up. Mr. Wouda had slouched into his chair. He looked as though he were dissolving into the upholstery. Mrs. Wouda was glaring at Marta, eyes and lips rigid.

Marta rose. "I know that nothing will bring Aaron back. But I still wanted you to know that I'm sorry."

MARTA DROVE along the country roads, turning randomly, letting herself get lost. Her flight did not leave for thirty-six hours, and there was nothing more to do. She supposed she should eat something before morning. Maybe one of the Lethbridge fast food places would still be open when she got back to her hotel. She felt no hurry. The Alberta sky vaulted above her, an enormous dome. The sun had melted into marbleized swirls and bands just above the prairie, casting enough light that the crops in the fields she passed were still easy to recognize: sugar beets, alfalfa, flax, canola. The sunflowers, with their bulky heads and lofty height, were especially distinctive. She remembered the first time she'd seen the plants when she was a girl. It was an uncommon crop at that time in southern Alberta. She'd accompanied her mother to buy eggs from the Vanderveens' chicken farm in June. "Are those potato plants?" she'd asked. "I guess so," her mother said, eyes on the road. Marta had nodded, but, even from the moving car, the leaves looked wrong. In early August, she travelled the same route with her mother, and the field was awash in bright yellow. Her mother stopped the car, and she and Marta stood at the edge of the field, gazing at the flowers and beaming at each other. "Wish I had a camera," her mother had said.

She scrutinized the irrigation systems that she passed. All farmers used them; southern Alberta could not count on enough rain for its crops. She remembered animated discussions among the farm kids in her science classes—they disagreed about whether farmers should save money by sticking to their old irrigation methods or upgrading to systems more efficient at controlling wind drift, runoff, and evaporation. She wondered if the sugar beet farmers still used what they called hood irrigation—simply cutting ditches through their fields and allowing them to flood. Most of the farmers in her father's congregation had used some sort of pipe or sprinkler system, but the sophistication varied, as did the amount of work the types required. The boys in her high school got summer jobs moving pipes by hand for the least advanced systems. Usually a stoic lot, they grumbled about the labour. It sounded miserable: dull, repetitive, and back-breaking. Other farmers had the motorized wheel-line systems—horizontal pipes on wheels that inched themselves across the fields and back. Marta passed a number of these. They looked like Meccano or K'nex sculptures: silhouettes of giant toys in the half-light.

She turned another corner at an alfalfa field where a pivot system was hard at work. During the last summer of Aaron's life, Mr. Wouda was installing pivot irrigation, a series of above-ground pipes and sprinklers that moved circularly, like the hands of a clock. They learned about the system in grade eleven physics. It covered a hundred and sixty acres at a time, and it ensured constant and consistent watering without the need to control how far the wheels would move in one direction, unlike the wheel-move method. Kids at school said that if you put your hand in front of a spigot, the force of the water would cut it off. To her knowledge, no one had tested that claim. But there were other tragedies related to irrigation in the area. The irrigation ditches were treacherous, with their slippery cement sides, the deep water. In late summer when she was eleven, the five-year-old son of a young couple in their church drowned in one of those ditches. Danny.

She pulled alongside the road and stopped the car. No traffic in sight. It was growing dark now. She watched a small group of Canada geese fly overhead. Why hadn't God arranged rescue for Danny? The little boy had come with his mother and his little sister, bringing lunch to his dad, who was harvesting the alfalfa. Lethbridge alfalfa was the best in the world, she'd heard people say. It was going to be a bumper crop that year—that's what the talk had been among the adults. Mr. Hoff had stopped the harvester to eat lunch with his wife. She pressed a sandwich into Danny's hands, but he wanted to play. They sat against the harvester's tires—it was a sunny day, but, as usual, very windy. And then, when they were, Marta imagined, surveying the harvest, enjoying each other's company, savouring the moment of rest, Danny wandered away. Wandered to the edge of the ditch and lost his balance. Drowned. That part was not her imagination. One moment. Bad luck. Where were God's hands?

Marta rolled down the window and stuck her head out into the fresh night air. The wind gusted, and she turned her head so that her hair, which, at last, was growing into longer wisps, blew backward, away from her eyes. For the most part, people needed to be the hands of God on earth. Occasionally one heard stories of angel visitations and supernatural rescue, and Marta believed them—after all, she was quite sure that God had sent her signs, personal signs. But mostly it was people who ministered to one another, people who rescued, intervened, advised, comforted. That's what she reminded herself of in her guidance counselling.

She considered the other tragic deaths. If she drove to the little graveyard near her old church, Aaron's grave would not be the only one that seemed dug too soon. John Klaason would be there too. He'd died after a field party. She hadn't been there—had been just a girl at the time. There had been a chinook—it had been ten or eleven degrees that day, and sunny. A bunch of teens arranged to meet in the laneway of the Bakemas' field to drink. John Klaason had passed out. No one noticed him—he lived one farm over, so they thought maybe he'd gone home. The temperatures that night plummeted to minus ten. Marta didn't know whether he'd died from alcohol poisoning or hypothermia.

Sandra Oudman would be there too. She'd died on Halloween in a prank gone wrong. Someone, or more likely a group of people, teens maybe, barricaded the road with hay bales. She had been driving home from her fiancé's, where they had handed out candy to the neighbourhood kids. And Natalie Agema was buried next to her grandfather—she died of a brain tumour at age fifteen. Then there were the other cancer deaths, farm accidents, premature births that became premature deaths. And that was just in her father's congregation. In the wider Lethbridge community, there was the usual assortment of pestilence and calamity. Occasionally, death came by violent hands—a beating, a strangling, a shooting. Other suicides occurred too—people stepped off the High Level Bridge, smashed into the ground some ninety-seven metres later.

Some deaths could have been postponed, but what of that? If you didn't die tragically, you would still die eventually. No one survived old age forever.

Night had gathered, and she drove the black band of road through darkness. Now she wanted to get back, back to the hotel for now, and back to Toronto too. She observed the night sky. It was a bowl of stars. She tried to imagine it as the inside of a hazelnut shell, envisioned the world as a hazelnut that God loved tenderly, vigilantly, as Dame Julian had seen in her vision. It wasn't her lack of faith, she thought, that prevented her from feeling God's love. She could accept Dame Julian's conviction—that the suffering would end in the fullness of time, that God's plans were well under way. All *would be* well. She believed that.

But she was living in the meantime, not the fullness of time, and the suffering was hard, hard to watch and hard to endure. People reeled from death. Loss walloped them, knocked the breath out of them. They lost their most basic appetites. They felt a desperate restlessness. Nothing gave them comfort or pleasure. Some never recovered; the grief flowed like molten lava, transforming the landscape of their hearts. Those were the ones like Mr. Wouda, who appeared to sleepwalk through the rest of their lives. And even those whose hearts were merely wounded were not stronger for having travelled through grief; they were marked by the journey, scarred and vulnerable.

And what if you were culpable? Partly to blame? You dragged the hay bale to the road. Took your eyes off your son, let him wander. Ignored the email that howled anger and despair. Could God really look on *you* with eyes of empathy and love?

And there was another problem. The perspective bewildered her. How could the world with all its problems be as little as a hazelnut? All the people in the world, last names *A* to *Z*. Not to mention the people who didn't have last names, whole tribes and cultures that didn't bother with surnames. If the world were hazelnut-sized to God, that made the people in it so tiny, so fragile.

In Sunday school, they had learned that not a hair could fall from their heads without God knowing. They had to memorize a Bible verse that said so: *Even the very hairs of your head are all numbered.* That suggested that God knew about her bad haircut. Knew and maybe even cared. There were sparrows in that passage too. They couldn't fall without God heeding. "*Fear not, therefore,*" her class had recited. You got a star sticker on the Sunday school chart if you knew your memory work. "*Ye are of more value than many sparrows.*" She tried to imagine a God so big that the world was nut-sized to him. Like a marble. And then she tried to imagine a God capable of loving each person and thing inside that little marble. Dame Julian was visited by God—he gave her visions of his love so vast and yet so precise that it reached each person. Marta recalled what Kathy had read to them about God's love being like sunlight. If you keep holding an umbrella up, you can't feel its warmth, she'd said.

She looked up at the cavernous sky and tried to fathom infinity. The stars glowed at her. She tried to fathom infinite love. It was impossible. But perhaps she could imagine love like light, love that glimmered through the night, reached across the galaxy to light her way.

It dawned on her then that if God loved her enough to send her a mink and a dove, a dove in Bathurst Station, maybe he loved her enough to forgive her.

WHEN SHE got to the hotel, she phoned Jenn.

"Marta, are you okay?" She sounded alarmed.

"Yeah, fine."

"Do you know what time it is?"

Marta glanced at the clock radio beside the bed. Just before 11:00 PM here meant just before 1:00 AM in Toronto. "Oh, sorry."

Long-suffering sigh. "How did the day go? What did you find out?"

"Nothing."

"Nothing?"

"Nothing."

"Did you see Mr. Maas?"

"Yes."

"Did you open the letter?"

"Yes. It said nothing."

"How—was it blank?"

"No. Just uninformative. I'll show you when I get home. Mr. Maas gave it to me."

"So you haven't seen Aaron's parents yet?"

"Yeah, I did."

"And?"

"Nothing. Nothing new. They blame me. Or at least Aaron's mom does."

"Bitch."

"Yeah, I suppose. I feel bad for her. It's like they're—just going through the motions. Everything looked the same, except older."

"Is Aaron's room still—Aaron's room?"

"I didn't go upstairs. Probably."

"Were they nasty to you?"

"Kind of. But it was okay. I didn't really care that much, after the initial shock."

"What do you mean?"

"This is going to sound weird. It was good to hear them confirm what I already thought. It was freeing."

SHE PHONED Matt next. If he was asleep, the fan in their bedroom, a cheap, noisy one, would drown out the ringing phone. They ran the fan all summer, since even with the window open their bedroom was stuffy.

"Marta."

"You're up."

"Yeah. I was out tonight."

"With who?"

"The Wheat Girls. Well, just Zara."

Marta considered hanging up the phone—not violently, just settling it back in its cradle, and then finding something else to do. She could watch TV. Go to the vending machines and buy pretzels and a Mars bar.

"Marta, there's nothing going on. She's engaged, or just about."

"Uh huh." Marta shifted the receiver to her other hand. "How's the cockroach situation?"

"The same. You've been gone less than one day."

He was right. Less than twenty-four hours. It seemed like a week, three weeks. "Seen any?"

"Two dead ones. The poison must be working."

"That's good."

"Marta, are we going to stay together?"

"I don't know." This time, her stomach didn't clench. She considered the question as if she were surveying a fork in the road, which meant it prompted her customary indecision. "If we do, things have to change. Not just me."

"I know."

"Should we talk about it when I get back?"

"Yeah. What about marriage counselling? Zara said she knew someone good."

Anger spread physically through Marta; she could feel her

cheeks warm at the thought of Matt discussing their marriage with the singer. "You'd need to find a job first, so that we could afford counselling. Stop pretending you're a musician when you don't even play an instrument. Maybe you should get that real estate licence you've been telling everyone about for years. Earn a living." She swung the words at him like barbed wire and felt bad almost immediately.

"Okay."

Okay? He sounded straight up. As happened so often, she wanted to believe him, to yield and to trust. But his love was shifting sand, and the foundation on which they'd built their life together was shakier than the houses built on ash heaps. Their marriage required repairs at its very root.

"We'll talk when I get home."

CHAPTER SIXTEEN

SHE MET KATHY IN THE building next door to the church, space that had been renovated to house offices and meeting rooms.

"Would you like a cup of tea?" Kathy was wearing grey dress pants, Birkenstocks, and an ivory blouse. Everything about her seemed calm, even the way her short, neat hair rested against her head.

While the tea steeped, Marta filled Kathy in on Aaron. Kathy listened, nodding from time to time. She asked questions: How old was he? How old was she? How long ago? How did he do it?

"Why do you want to know that?"

Kathy looked pensive. "I think that the method someone chooses can reveal how serious they are, how strong their death wish is. Sometimes, it suggests that they want to hurt others through their death or make a statement. But you probably know more about suicide than I do—in your line of work, I mean."

"I know a bit about suicide prevention. Luckily not that much about suicide. I've dealt with suicidal students, but I haven't lost one yet." Knock on wood. Not that she believed in that superstition.

"It's providential that you're there for those students. The grace of God acting in that school."

Marta's disbelief must have been visible because Kathy said, "No, I mean it. Maybe if Aaron had had an adult like you—someone with good training and insight and concern, he would have gotten the help he needed."

Marta recalled Christine Vanderpool for the second time in a week. She hadn't thought about the guidance counsellor in years, since moving to Toronto, probably. Maybe Mrs. Vanderpool had meant well, but she was of little use. Worse than Marta. Aside from her propensity for gossip, she blared advice when you visited her small office. Marta didn't know of anyone who had visited her voluntarily. Just the annual compulsory visit for course selection. Sometimes troublesome students got sent to Mrs. Vanderpool for a talking-to about where their behaviour would take them. Aaron's friend Dylan could do an admirable imitation of that lecture, mimicking the way Mrs. Vanderpool arched her back and lurched her large bosom forward in emphasis.

It had not occurred to Marta that Mrs. Vanderpool could have, perhaps even should have, caught Aaron's warning signs. Mental illness had such stigma that it was rarely discussed. In fact, some people in the community felt that it was a sign of inadequate faith. When her mother's Bible study group met at their house, she'd heard one of the women say that depression showed ingratitude. "If you just live your life in praise of God and his wondrous works, how could you be depressed?" Her mother had objected, but Marta grew up understanding that her parents' positions on a range of topics were suspect.

Marta's head had been tilting up and down while she reflected. She stilled it and addressed Kathy. "I think it was a community that let some people fall through cracks. If I had been struggling there, with mental illness, I mean, I would have done my best not to let people know."

"So he was a teenaged boy—a subgroup rather known for its lack of self-expression. He was from a Dutch background, a culture known for its reserve—forgive me if I'm stereotyping. And part of a religious community that taught its members to soldier on when they felt bad. Do I have it right?"

"Pretty much."

Kathy nodded, the pensive expression back on her face. "I doubt very much that there was a moment when you could have acted to prevent the tragedy. Or a moment when you should have held your tongue or refrained from acting. It's just not that simple. Even if you had emailed him back, you don't know that that would have prevented his death. Even if you hadn't broken up with him, he may still have taken his life."

Marta had been studying Kathy's face, scrutinizing her expression for any hint of insincerity. Now she realized she was still staring, though Kathy had finished speaking. She pulled her eyes away. She took a breath. She was a prisoner who had unexpectedly found herself at a parole board hearing. Maybe not *unexpectedly*—she had booked this appointment with Kathy. She took a few more breaths. She tried to keep her expression neutral. It shouldn't matter so much after all these years, an almost-stranger's opinion of her actions and inactions from more than a decade before.

"You think I might not have made a difference?"

Kathy's voice was frank and composed. "Whatever was going on with him, he didn't share it with you or with anyone else, by the sounds of it. He certainly didn't tell you his intentions. If it was mental illness, that's a dark force, even more dangerous when it's kept hidden."

Marta mulled that over. Her counsellor-self knew how true that was—how difficult it was to help someone whose thinking was skewed, and whose will was focused on concealing the problem. But did it absolve her? If this was a parole hearing, she was being offered not only freedom but pardon. It seemed too good to be true. The prospect dazzled her, disoriented her, like the brilliant sunlight the time she and Oliver had emerged from a tunnel in the early afternoon.

"That's what my sister says. And my parents. That Aaron's life wasn't in my hands." She listened to the words as she spoke them, and they hummed with possibility. A month ago, they would have sounded like a bald-faced lie, as false as if she had announced she had been skydiving or owned a pet iguana. Now she considered taking the burden of her culpability, her alleged culpability, and simply laying it down. Leaving it by the side of the road and striding forward unencumbered.

"So often we don't have control over the outcomes—not in other people's lives, at least. Not even in our own, sometimes. That knowledge can be hard to live with."

"You think those situations are in God's hands, though?" Because, if it wasn't her fault, whose fault was it?

"I don't know why terrible things happen. I don't have an explanation for Aaron's death." She touched Marta's arm with her fingers. "But it's time for you to forgive yourself, Marta.

This doesn't really have to do with God. God has never held you responsible."

MARTA PAUSED on her way home. The corner of Bloor and Dovercourt looked as shabby as ever. Maybe even a little worse. A middle-aged woman in a one-piece bathing suit that strained around her middle was panhandling in front of the We Fight Your Traffic Tickets office. Her dog, a large-breed brown mutt, panted on the pavement. It looked hot and thirsty.

Despite the panorama around her, Marta felt what she thought must be peace. It was unfamiliar to her, this emotion. She thought of a photograph she'd seen on the wall in Drift just a few blocks away. It showed a line of police officers in full riot gear. In front of them was a young man, a demonstrator, looking composed, even happy. He held a sign that read EVERYTHING IS OK. For the moment, for Marta, it was. She thought of the grace she had received.

Grace was the sort of gift that came with no obligation, no expectation of reciprocation. It wasn't good fortune, like winning the raffle or being caller number nine. It was a deliberate act, an act that flowed from kindness and generosity. She remembered witnessing it a few years before when she and Jenn had volunteered at the Scott Mission serving hot meals. There was a man who came in agitated. Shoved away the cup of yogourt and the juice boxes in front of him. Sent back the first plate of food, told Jenn he was vegetarian. "Is that a good idea, when you're homeless?" Jenn murmured to Marta on her way back to the kitchen.

The vegetarian meal was the same plate minus the meat. No protein anywhere. Next he fussed about the bread. Noticed that there were only brown rolls in his table's basket, but other tables had white buns. "What am I—goddamn second class!?" Marta stood back, intimidated by his aggression. "For God's sake, it's free food," Jenn muttered in Marta's ear. Another volunteer, a tiny Asian woman who had been so quiet that Marta wondered if she spoke English, strode to a nearby table with only two guests at it. She said something to them, gestured toward their bread basket and the man at Marta's table. She picked up two white rolls with a clean napkin, came to the agitated man, and slipped them next to his plate. "Here you are, sir." Then she slipped away to begin clearing dishes at a table where the guests had finished. She didn't wait to see the man's expression, or pause to see if he would thank her. Just met his need with the speed, the directness, the lack of judgment you would use to return a fallen toy to a baby.

Marta knew she had been offered grace before—certainly from her parents, especially her father, who had worked hard to help her after Aaron's death. But his love for her biased him, and she couldn't trust the clemency he offered. It seemed indulgent, overly optimistic, as unreliable as your mother telling you you're beautiful.

Kathy, on the other hand, barely knew her and had nothing at stake.

Or maybe it was about timing and distance, the journey she had to complete. "It's time," Kathy had said. Time to forgive herself. She felt as though she had traversed numerous landscapes, travelled along roads and through tunnels to come first to Kathy's office, then here, to the dingy corner of Bloor and Dovercourt. The place was familiar, but she saw it with new eyes. She had entered a new room—larger, more open—and her relief was physical, as when both body and soul relax after escaping the tug and roar of the crowd and arriving at home.

A couple of pigeons landed on a bike rack in front of the dollar store. Marta watched as one ruffled its wings. She knew now what the mink and her dove had been telling her. "Really?" she could hear Jenn say. Or maybe just, "Oh, Marta."

Her eyes strayed to the manhole cover at the edge of the street. She pictured what lay beneath her: the wide storm drain running east to Delaware Avenue, the sanitary sewer, the subway. She turned her head up to the sunlit sky. Planets, the galaxy, somewhere a heaven. The world, she felt, swelled with mystery and possibility.

THE THURSDAY before Labour Day was sunny, with temperatures in the low twenties, the kind of weather that made Marta long to be outside. But an unending line of students, some registering, most making course changes, had kept Marta occupied well into the afternoon. Only the guidance counsellors and administrators had to be in school before the long weekend, and it was a tedious week, sorting through schedules, noting prerequisites, filling out the paperwork. Finally, she was free. She took the subway to High Park, where she'd arranged to meet Jenn for one last summer walk before the schedule of another school year took over.

Jenn was waiting at the northeast corner of the park. "Did you know that when a work crew was expanding storm pools here, they set off a geyser?" Marta said. "A huge geyser—fifteen metres high."

"Hello to you too. What caused it?"

"The Laurentian River. It flows deep in the bedrock all the way from Georgian Bay. The water's red because of all the iron in it. It stains everything. That's why the concrete is red." She pointed at the stormwater pond they were passing.

"Is that what comes out of the drinking fountains in the park? I'm bringing my own water from now on."

"No, it has salt in it too, so it's no good for drinking or even for watering the gardens here."

"So do they use water from Grenadier for the fountains?" Jenn pointed westward toward the pond down the hill, and her nose wrinkled as if they were passing fresh manure.

"Hey! A lot of work's been done recently to restore that pond. And I'm sure what comes out of the water fountains in the park is as good as the water from your tap at home."

"Let's go see how polluted it looks."

"Fine with me."

It was a steep descent, and muddy from the rain the night before. Marta stopped for a minute to consider taking off her shoes—her black flats were a mainstay of her outfits for work. But the roots and rocks would hurt her feet. Her fingers moved to her palm. She stopped them. Decided the shoes could be cleaned. Reminded herself of her New Year's resolution to be more decisive. It wasn't January, but for staff and students, the new school year felt like more of a fresh start than the real New Year.

"How's your week going?" asked Jenn.

"It's kind of crazy but good."

"I still think you should have applied for that job you told me about—in Etobicoke."

"It wasn't for me." Marta thought back to her day. Around eleven o'clock that morning, she'd spotted Mercedes and an older woman with the same thin face and wide, expressive eyes. They were halfway down the line, probably had been waiting a half-hour or more. "Do you mind if I see that parent next?" she had murmured to the students in the front of the line.

She'd ushered Mercedes and the woman into her office, pushed the door almost closed.

"How are you, Mercedes?"

"Better. I'm seeing a shrink. A psychologist." The girl avoided Marta's eyes.

The woman had been watching Mercedes. She spoke in fast Spanish, the tone admonishing. She held the girl's wrist and gave it a little shake. The action was more tender than violent.

"My mother doesn't speak English. She wants me to say thank you—from her—for helping me." The girl looked uneasy, embarrassed.

"You're welcome. Tell your mother she's welcome. It's what I'm here for. I'm so glad you're doing better. Have you signed up for classes this fall?"

"Yeah. I wanna switch out of Mrs. Gianni's English class though. I hear she yells a lot."

"We don't usually let students switch out of classes because they don't like the teacher. But I'll see what I can do. Come see me on Tuesday." She smiled at Mercedes, and though the girl didn't quite smile back, she did meet Marta's eyes this time. Behind the discomfort, there was vitality that had been absent in June. Marta felt relieved. She stood to usher them out. "Thank you for coming." She addressed the mother.

"*Muchísimas gracias.*" The mother clutched Marta's wrist with the same tenderness with which she had grasped her daughter's, and there were tears in her eyes.

Marta and Jenn had reached the bottom of the hill and were walking south along a paved trail now, wide enough to walk side by side. The pond glimmered on their right. "Look—there's a heron!" Marta pointed beyond the reeds where a great blue heron stood on its impossibly narrow legs, fishing in the late afternoon sun. "Gorgeous!"

"Have you heard about the peregrine falcons on the top of the Sheraton downtown?"

"Yeah—the ones with live-action cameras on them. You can watch them 24-7."

"I didn't know that. On the Internet?"

"Yep."

"Cool."

"They're the reason I'm staying at Dufferin Tech."

Jenn stopped and turned to look at Marta.

"I thought about it—those baby falcons, needing help to survive."

"You think your kids are like baby peregrine falcons?"

Marta had already braced herself for Jenn's skepticism. "I don't mean their parents are bad. But some of them have had a rough time. They could use help. Even my help. Besides, my heart was made to love my neighbourhood. I like that it's a place that wears its dysfunction on the outside, if you know what I mean. I get suspicious of anything too pretty or too polished."

Jenn nodded slowly, as if she were considering Marta's statements one by one and approving them individually. After a moment she said, "Okay. How are you and Matt doing?"

Marta looked out on the pond. Once or twice a year, the temperature dipped low enough for long enough that you could skate on the pond. It wasn't exactly legal, but Marta went anyway. It thrilled her to step onto a surface that one couldn't traverse the rest of the year, at least not on foot. A few years ago frigid air had settled over the city without bringing snow. Marta soared all over the ice, north to south, east to west. It was like skating on the sloughs in Lethbridge—no people to avoid, just space on all sides, sky above, thick ice, and deep water below.

Marta looked at Jenn. "Do you remember that legend about the pond—we heard it during Doors Open in Colborne Lodge?"

"About the grenadiers from Fort York that drowned in the pond?"

"Yeah, and you can sometimes see their hands pushing up from underneath the ice in the winter."

"Sounds like a load of crap."

"Jenn, you have no imagination."

"You have far too much imagination."

Marta considered the pond again. She had no trouble imagining being trapped under the ice—she knew how it would feel. She gazed around her, felt the sunlight, glorious on her face, heard the raucous cries of the red-winged blackbirds, watched the heron take flight and soar low across the water.

"I don't know what's going to happen with Matt and me. We start seeing a marriage counsellor next week. Kathy—you know, the priest from St. Anne's—recommended one."

"Are you feeling hopeful?"

"Not really. Maybe we can move forward. I feel ready to make changes, but I don't know about him. I'll give it a try, though." She meant it. She *would* work at it, although it was tempting to leave him, almost heady to imagine just parting ways. She could test this new strength she felt and see if her hunch was right. She thought her fear was gone. And if it was, she didn't need Matt to help her stave it off anymore, if that's what his presence in her life was doing. She thought about a story she'd read in an old *Glamour* magazine at the dentist's office a week ago. It featured before-and-after photos of an obese woman who exercised and dieted until she achieved supermodel slenderness. "I was empowered!" said the caption underneath the thin version of the woman. The story applauded the woman for casting off first the pounds and then the people and situations that encumbered her—including her abusive boyfriend. Maybe their situations were similar, Marta had reflected, examining the woman's radiant smile in the after photo. But Matt was not abusive, and leaving a marriage was not necessarily an act of empowerment. One never really just walked away—she knew that. Marriage wove its own cocoon around a couple over time, the threads composed of all their conversations both meaningful and trivial, of the embraces, the routines, the shared memories, the intimacy and holiness of bearing witness to each other's lives. When she imagined unravelling all of that, the headiness she felt at the thought of leaving dissipated. So maybe they could find each other again. At least they could try. Maybe they'd even have a baby someday. But that was getting ahead of things. She'd see how the counselling went.

Jenn squeezed Marta's hand. "Let me know if there's anything I can do."

"Thanks."

"Hey, did you ever open your own letter—the one Mr. Maas sent to you?"

So many questions, Marta thought, but she felt a rush of fondness for her sister. "Yeah, I did. It was what I remembered. Short and shallow."

"What did it say?"

Marta recalled the loopy purple script. *Dear Marta of the Future: I hope you are doing okay.* Then the young Marta had listed what she thought "okay" should look like: *I hope you are a famous singer. I hope people stop you for autographs and tell you what a difference you make. I hope you're married to great guy who thinks you're amazing . . .*

"She said she hoped I was doing all right. That's all, really. I put it away to open again in thirteen years. I might even write another letter to open with it." Marta turned toward loud chatter in the oak tree next to them—a squirrel scolding someone, maybe Marta and Jenn themselves for interrupting its acorn harvest. The dappled sunlight danced in leafy patterns on the path, and Marta found herself smiling. "I think that squirrel wants us to move along. Let's keep walking." She took Jenn's hand and swung it.

A teenaged girl skateboarded past them, her golden retriever loping beside her. In the pond, mallards and wood ducks were toppling forward, rumps in the air as they nibbled the wetland plants just below the water's surface. A lawnmower hummed in the distance, which reminded Marta of her song—maybe she'd have another go at it on the weekend. She breathed in the smell of freshly cut grass, mingled with more pungent scents—the reeds, the fish, probably some goose poop too. The crickets and cicadas piped their late-summer symphony. Some seagulls overhead added their squeaks and squawks. And somewhere very close, though she had to strain to hear them above all the other noise, there were rock doves crooning their low, steady songs.

EPILOGUE

THE REVEREND JACOB ELZINGA HAS been fading in and out of consciousness. But he knows that the bed he is lying in is his death bed. He can feel it from the scratchy sheets with their hospital smell, not the air-dried freshness of the sheets he and Winnie hang on their clothesline to dry. He can tell from the way the hospital chaplain holds tight to his hand as he prays with him, from the solemnity in the chaplain's tone.

The girls will look after Winnie. They all suspected he would die first, given his heart condition. A few years ago, he and Winnie added their names to the wait list at the Holland Home in Brampton, less than an hour from Toronto. Winnie will make connections there quickly, find out who is related to people in their former congregations, who is their own distant relative. The insularity of the Dutch Christian Reformed community that has irked him over the years will serve her well when he is gone. And, of course, the girls will be near Winnie. They'll visit.

The girls. They've been visiting him, but they're not here now. He doesn't know what to do about them, or for them. Jenn with her independence, doing everything her own way. The hard way, though she would disagree. But no sooner has she scaled the heights of a human resources department than she switches firms, seeking out larger and more complex workplaces. Each time—her voice on the phone confident and matter of fact—she asserts that the move is financially strategic and timed for optimal job security. "There's always a risk," she told him last March when she accepted the job at Global Tech, "but it's calculated." No leaps of faith for his Jenn.

He shifts, unsure whether the cramping he's feeling is from body or soul. He turns his head away from the chaplain, who is still praying, long, winding phrases about transgressions and forgiveness and the abundant love of our merciful Father in heaven. At least Jenn has found someone to share her life. Jacob was not well enough to officiate at the wedding in August, but he was able to attend. He twitches and feels the chaplain squeeze his hand in response. Marta told him about the seventeen-page prenuptial agreement Jenn had Eloi sign. Detail after detail regarding the "what ifs" that could come their way. Has he failed Jenn? Her combination of cautiousness and restlessness might be because of him—maybe he raised her to feel unsafe.

And Marta. The ways he has fallen short where she is concerned. Aaron's death, for instance. He, a pastor, could not bring her peace or closure. How his heart protested when she set off to visit Aaron's embittered, broken parents a few years ago. He recalls the day he learned of her plans. "Don't go," he said, or something like that, something clear and blunt. But his words wafted through the phone line, just ineffectual electronic impulses. He spent the night in his chair. As the sun rose, he imagined Marta in a taxi speeding down the 401 to the airport. He remembers how he wanted to hurl himself in front of the plane or her rental car or the Woudas' front door, his arms up to signal "Halt!" He imagined scooping her up like a toddler about to topple, planting her far away from danger. But he is no superhero. His arms, always on the thin side, have been withered and shrunken for years. So he stayed put, fretted in his chair, muttering prayers while his beloved daughter marched toward calamity.

The chaplain has finished his prayer with a loud "Amen," loud enough to startle Jacob. The tube in Jacob's throat prevents conversation, but Jacob considers opening his eyes, perhaps trying to signal with his expression and a little flutter of his fingers that the chaplain can go. He decides there is too much potential for misinterpretation—the chaplain will think Jacob wants something. He'll offer water, ask if he's in pain, does he need the nurse, does he want Winnie. It's too much. Jacob lies still.

He would like to see Marta one last time. To confirm that she's all right. He's pretty sure she is all right. He remembers her visit from a year or so ago. She came to stay with Winnie and him for a long weekend, right after Jenn got engaged. "Looks like not only will we be visiting Toronto for the wedding, but we'll also be moving back there," he announced. "Your mother has requested the next available space at the home for the decrepit Dutch. The Holland Home for the Hobbling."

Winnie had entered the room with a tray of mugs and a teapot. She gave him a look just short of a glare. Marta said, "Don't call it that." But she was sucking in her cheeks to hold back a smile. "That's in Brampton. You know we Torontonians don't consider that Toronto." Her voice became cautious. "Do you ever wish we had moved to Toronto the first time you got the call? Or maybe never moved there at all?"

He remembers the guilt her words induced. Like the time Jenn—at maybe ten years old—had found him lighting his pipe during her school's anti-smoking campaign week. Later, she'd slipped a handmade poster on his desk. *Reasons Why You Should Quit Smoking.* The list started with her and Marta's names.

"Sometimes we've talked about it—that it would have been better to move when you and Jenn were younger—an easier adjustment for you. Maybe . . ." He glanced over at Winnie, who was gazing at Marta, eyes sympathetic. When she caught Jacob's look, there was still benevolence in her face, but her mouth got that disapproving tilt to it again. She turned her attention to the tea she was pouring. Perhaps he would have been a wiser man if she had challenged him more over the years. Or even if she had challenged him as much when the girls were little as she did now. He turned back to Marta and noticed, for the second or third time since she'd arrived, her stillness. She seemed calm. Even as she waited for him to elaborate, there was more curiosity than anxiety in her eyes.

"I thought it was the right choice. In fact, I thought it was the will of God. But maybe I should have given it more thought. Talked about it with your mother a bit more. And even with you and Jenn, little as you were back then." He couldn't hold back a sigh. "I just don't know. I guess after all these years, I'm still not entirely sure how God works his will on earth."

Marta simply nodded. Then she said, "I've decided not to apply for the department head position in guidance."

"I didn't know you were thinking about it," said her mother. She handed Marta and Jacob mugs of tea and sat down in the armchair next to him.

"I wasn't really—I just mentioned it to Jenn, and she's been pressuring me to go for it. More money, more prestige. Not that there's actually money or prestige to be had in my line of work. That's just Jenn's opinion."

Jacob heard the wry confidence in her voice. He looked at her hands. One cupped the mug of tea, the other rested in her lap like a cat.

The chaplain's voice startles Jacob. "Would you like me to read some scripture to you before I leave? Maybe one of the psalms?" Jacob hears pages fluttering. He wonders what passage the chaplain will choose for a dying man. Jacob is not a gambling man—that is, not the kind of gambling that involves money. But if he were, he would bet on the chaplain choosing Psalm 23. Though he paid little attention to the prayer—God forgive him—he noticed his lack of surprise at its content and phrasing. Ah, well, Psalm 23 is popular because it's comforting. A fitting passage for someone at death's door.

Jacob's thoughts shift. Will he go to heaven? He longs to hear God say, "Thou good and faithful servant." Take his hand and welcome him. But he is unworthy. God could say, "You buried your talent in the cold Canadian ground. I gave you gifts, and you were passive. Ungrateful. Afraid. And you tested me." And that is all true. "Not exactly a giant of faith, are you?" He searches for a defence against this version of God he has conjured.

He wishes he had told Marta and Jenn about that Nazi soldier, the one from that night of his childhood. That soldier has lurked in Jacob's subconscious all these years; he is like an odour in the back of a crowded fridge, something grim that Jacob has lacked the nerve to expose or to examine. Jacob has told his children almost nothing about the Nazi occupation. Jenn tried to wrench information from him more than once, but he deflected the questions—told her he had been too young to have retained clear memories. Few of the Dutch immigrants talk about the war. The silence, he knows, is part of the coping style, a cultural thing. "No point in dwelling on the miseries of the past."

He wonders now whether or not withholding the events of his past has made anything easier or better. Maybe if he had told his children about the trauma he endured, about his fear and shame, it would have helped his daughters understand him—and, in turn, themselves—more fully. They would understand how helpless and how powerless he felt. And maybe even how those childhood experiences, or, more accurately, the feelings that permeated those childhood experiences, inhibited him for years to come. Or maybe that was just an excuse—blaming his early years for his lack of confidence and his meekness. When he counselled troubled parishioners as part of his pastoral work, he gave their heartaches his full attention, but he also explained to them that one can't go on using past trauma to justify deficiencies in the present. Now he wonders whether or not he ever followed his own advice.

It was the shame mostly, he thinks now, that harmed him. He hadn't been too young to form lasting memories of those war events, but he had been too young to be trusted with information, and, at the time, he didn't grasp *why* his father was in hiding. He assumed his father had done something wrong. It wasn't until the war was over that Jacob learned about the Dutch Resistance—and that he should be proud of his father, and proud of his mother too. She managed the house and farm while his father passed on counterintelligence and distributed the underground press. Or at least that's what his father *may* have been doing. He still doesn't know for sure, since his father also believed in silences. His father did not exactly forbid questions about the war, but he was like a tap that dribbled lukewarm water. The experience of extracting information was both slow and unsatisfactory, and his children soon learned that it was not worth the effort. Jacob's thoughts grow quiet.

The chaplain is reading now. Uh huh. "*The Lord is my shepherd. I shall not want.*" Jacob feels no joy in being right. He decides to use the time he has left to heave a prayer for his children. He moves his lips, the better to express his love and longing. The chaplain lays a hand on Jacob's shoulder. "Yes, join me," he says. He intones King David's familiar consolation: "*Yea, though I walk through the valley of the shadow of death . . .*"

But the Reverend Jacob Elzinga is moving his tongue to describe his own valleys. He feels perplexed by his life, overwhelmed by all that is out of his hands now. Was it ever in his hands? He hears a snippet of the psalm again. David's psalm, the king who made cruel choices, bad mistakes, tested God. Yet there is certainty in his words. "*Thou art with me.*"

The Reverend Jacob Elzinga, still baffled but no longer afraid, moves his lips in counterpoint to the psalm that the chaplain recites. He climbs from the valley of the shadow of death. Decides it is too late to worry about the paths of righteousness. The old man is back in his mother's arms, hiding his eyes in her neck, feeling safe as he hears her put their safety in the hands of God. *"Thy will is done."*

ACKNOWLEDGMENTS

For me, one of the pleasures of writing a book is the research: the library trips, the web searches, and especially the consultations that entail my getting to know new people or getting to know old friends better. For information on the geography and geology of west-end Toronto, I thank Richard Anderson, who spent a cold February morning walking with me and describing what lies beneath the ground in the Bloor-Dufferin area. For geographical details about Lethbridge, I thank Harry and Joanne Boessenkool and Mark Lavorato. Any errors in the descriptions of settings are mine. Thank you to Jesse Weeks for consulting with me about police procedures and to Rob Crosby-Shearer for the tour of St. Anne's Anglican Church. I'm also grateful to the authors of the very informative essays in *HTO: Toronto's Water from Lake Iroquois to Lost Rivers to Low-flow Toilets*, edited by Wayne Reeves and Christina Palassio. I'd like to acknowledge two useful websites: infiltration.org, especially *Infiltration: The Zine About Going Places You're Not Supposed to Go*, and vanishingpoint.ca, a website created and maintained by Michael Cook. And an exuberant thank you to Robin Koke, my consultant and co-explorer of subterranean Toronto.

For help in understanding the teachings of Julian of Norwich, I thank Robert Sweetman. I also freely borrowed interpretations from Frederick Christian Bauerschmidt's article "Will Everything Really Be OK? The Spirituality of Julian of Norwich" (*Commonweal*, February 27, 1998), and I thank Dr. Bauerschmidt for his insight and clarity. Robert Llewelyn's books on Dame Julian were another valuable resource.

It was a pleasure to work with my editor, Robert Schreur, and I am grateful for his keen eye and his wisdom. For their thoughtful responses to early drafts, and for cheerleading me through the writing process, I thank Susan Cockerton and Douglas Burnet Smith.

Thank you to my publisher, Ruth Linka, for her belief in this project, and to the whole team at Brindle & Glass for the magic of turning a Word document into a lovely book. To Ruth, Cailey Cavallin, Pete Kohut, and Emily Shorthouse, I appreciate your hard work and your commitment to quality. Thank you to Heather Sangster at Strong Finish for careful proofreading.

I'd like to thank my colleagues at St. Clement's School and all the friends who have supported and encouraged me in the writing of this novel.

Finally, a thank you to Peryn and Tessa, who have put up with Mom writing another book. And love and thanks to Douglas Romanow—for the gift of time, for listening, for more listening, and for believing in me.

PATRICIA WESTERHOF was born to Dutch Canadian parents and has lived in the Netherlands, rural Alberta, and Ontario. She is the author of *Catch Me When I Fall*, a collection of linked stories, and co-author of *The Writer's Craft*, a textbook for creative writing students. Her short stories have been published in *Room Magazine*, the *Dalhousie Review*, and the anthology *Trees Running Backward*. Patricia lives in Toronto, where she teaches English and creative writing. Please visit patriciawesterhof.com.